D0287567

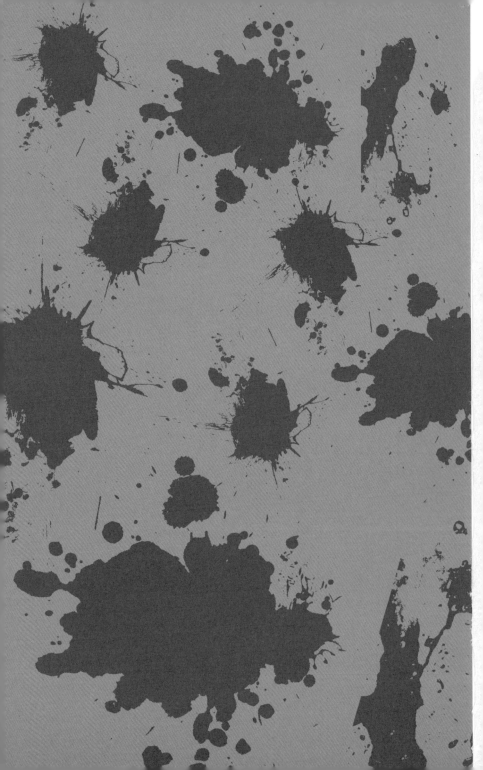

GARBAGE PAIL KIDS™

CAMP DAZE

BY
R.L. STINE

ALSO AVAILABLE BY R.L. STINE

Welcome to Smellville

Thrills and Chills

Illustrated by **JEFF ZAPATA**

Inks by **FRED WHEATON**

AMULET BOOKS • NEW YORK

R.L. STINE

GARBAGE PAIL KIDS™

CAMP DAZE

Cataloging-in-Publication Data has been applied for and may be obtained from the Library of Congress.

ISBN 978-1-4197-4365-8
Signed edition ISBN 978-1-4197-5999-4

By R.L. Stine
Interior illustrations by Jeff Zapata, Fred Wheaton, and Chris Meeks
Cover art by Joe Simko
Book design by Brenda E. Angelilli

Printed and bound in the United States
10 9 8 7 6 5 4 3 2 1

Amulet Books are available at special discounts when purchased in quantity for premiums and promotions as well as fundraising or educational use. Special editions can also be created to specification. For details, contact specialsales@abramsbooks.com or the address below.

ABRAMS The Art of Books
195 Broadway, New York, NY 10007
abramsbooks.com

"We're not
bad kids.
We just don't
know any
better."

Thanks once again go to the best friends of the Garbage
Pail Kids, Ira Friedman of Topps and Charlie Kochman
of Abrams. I couldn't write these books without their
knowledge, advice, and good (gross and ghastly) humor.

Meet the

GARBAGE PAIL KIDS™

ADAM BOMB

BABBLING BROOKE

BRAINY JANEY

CRANKY FRANKIE

HANDY **SANDY**

JUNKFOOD **JOHN**

LUKE PUKE

NERVOUS **REX**

ROB SLOB

WACKY **JACKIE**

ONE

Welcome, everyone. I'm Adam Bomb, and I think I might **E-X-P-L-O-D-E** with excitement. I'm warming my hands by a fire along with my nine friends. We are sitting in a circle watching the flames crackle and dance.

I don't know what you've heard about us, but the stories are all true. The ten of us live in a big, old house—all by ourselves—in the town of Smellville.

We don't know where our parents went.

We don't know how we all arrived in the house together.

And we don't know much of anything.

But we don't care—because we have such a good time.

And now we're all going to summer camp together.

We hear that Camp Lemme-Owttahere is a total blast.

Someone told us that 80 percent of the campers survive the summer. That sounds like pretty good odds to us.

We are so pumped, we've read all about the camp. Did you know that Camp Lemme-Owttahere is the only summer camp where kids can learn meat-processing?

Awesome!

Junkfood John is so excited. He said, "Just think. By the end of summer, we'll all be making our own bacon and sausages."

Babbling Brooke can't wait for the horseback riding. Sadly, the camp's horse died last summer. But we're still allowed to ride it.

Isn't that something?

Brainy Janey wants to study birds at camp. "Most birds live in cages," Janey told us. "But some birds live in the wild."

Brainy Janey knows everything. She's so smart, she can read in the dark.

"Did you know there are at least six different kinds of birds in the world?" she said. "Most of them are canaries. But there are other kinds, too."

"I once saw a Philadelphia Eagle," Wacky Jackie said. "He didn't look like a bird at all. He was wearing a helmet and shoulder pads. I wrote it up for science class."

You never know *what* Jackie will say. Most of the time, her words are well worth ignoring.

"I sewed a dress out of bird feathers once," Handy Sandy said. She's so handy. "But I couldn't wear it because I'm ticklish. Also, I'm allergic to feathers."

"Did you get a rash?" Nervous Rex asked her.

"No," she replied. "But my whole body broke out in big red spots."

Don't ask.

Handy Sandy has been saving up boxes of tissues because she has big plans for camp. "I want to build my own canoe out of tissues," she told us. "I just have to figure out how to make them waterproof."

Even Cranky Frankie is looking forward to summer camp. Frankie is so cranky, he shouts at himself in the mirror. He complains about everything. In fact, he once complained that his nose was on too tight.

Now *that's* cranky.

"I can't wait to tell the camp chef how lousy his food is!" Frankie declared. "I'm going to start complaining about our cabin even before we see it. And why do I have to wear wet sneakers every day?"

I squinted at him. "Frankie, why will your sneakers be wet?"

"I don't know," he answered. "But just thinking about it makes me cranky."

As you can see, we are all eager to get to Camp Lemme-Owttahere. Everyone, that is, except for Nervous Rex.

Rex doesn't want to go to camp. "The outdoors makes me nervous," he told us. "I was once bitten by a tree."

So, here we are sitting around a practice campfire. Darkness all around us. Bright yellow and orange flames leaping high. The heat feels good on my cheeks.

Camp doesn't start till next week, but I thought a practice campfire would help put us all in the mood.

I didn't know it would go so wrong.

TWO

We wanted to build a big campfire that we could all sit around, but we couldn't find any firewood.

"Firewood was invented in 1925," Brainy Janey told us. "Before that, people had to burn stones. They discovered that wood was a lot easier to light—especially after matches were invented in 1955."

Janey knows everything, but I'm not so sure everything she says is true.

We always have a lot of matches around because Cranky Frankie often threatens to set our parrot on fire.

That sounds cruel. But Ptooey, our dumb parrot, is always asking for it. Whenever Frankie comes near, Ptooey lifts one leg and squawks, **"Awwwk. Come over here. I've got a special-delivery present to deliver to your face!"**

Cranky Frankie tells the parrot to shut his yap.

"Awwwk," Ptooey squawks. **"Want to improve your looks? I'll peck your head off!"**

That's when Frankie usually goes for the matches.

"How can we build a campfire without firewood?" Babbling Brooke asked.

Of course, Handy Sandy had an answer. "We can use furniture," she said. "Tables and chairs will burn nicely."

She was right. A few minutes later, we had a blazing fire.

"Get the hot dogs," I said. "It's important to roast hot dogs around a campfire. This is an awesome practice. Like we'll be doing at camp."

"Uh . . . there's just one problem, Adam," Junkfood John said.

"Problem?" I asked.

He nodded. "I ate all the hot dogs as an after-dinner snack."

Luke Puke swallowed loudly. "But . . . John . . . those hot dogs were *raw!*" he said.

John shrugged. "I *thought* they were a little chewy!"

Luke made an **ULLLP** sound. He then grabbed his belly and ran to the bathroom.

"We can send for some pizza," Rob Slob said. "Then we can burn the boxes." He sat across the fire from me. The bright flames danced over his face.

"I like your new shirt, Rob," I told him. "All that green fringe hanging on the front looks really awesome."

"I'm not wearing a shirt," Rob said.

Perhaps Rob Slob needs a bath. But no one wants to be the one to tell him.

Babbling Brooke jumped to her feet. "I want to do my summer camp cheer," she announced. Brooke wants to be a cheerleader. She writes cheers for everything. Last week, she wrote a cheer for when her shoelace tore.

Brooke clapped her hands. "Here goes!" she cried. "I haven't quite finished it, but it's almost ready."

She leaped into the air and started her cheer:

"SUMMER CAMP! SUMMER
    CAMP!
"YOU'RE SO SOMETHING.
"YAY, CAMP. WHY DO I LOVE
    IT?
"BECAUSE SOMETHING
"SOMETHING SOMETHING
    SOMETHING.
"YAAAAY, CAMP!"

Brooke did a high cartwheel and landed with a **THUD** on her head. We all heard her skull crack. But it didn't seem to bother her.

"I know . . . my cheer still needs some work," she said. "I'm going to finish it before camp starts."

The bright orange flames stretched higher. The fire crackled and popped.

"At camp," Brainy Janey said, "kids sit around the campfire at night and tell ghost stories." She gazed around our circle. "Does anyone know a good ghost story?"

We all thought about it.

"I know a story," Wacky Jackie said. "But it doesn't have a ghost in it."

"I used to know a good ghost story," Rob Slob said. "But I forgot how it goes."

Nervous Rex hugged himself. "I-I don't like ghost stories," he stammered. "You have to be *dead* to be a ghost—don't you?"

"Yes, most ghosts are dead," I told him.

"W-well, that makes me nervous," Rex said. "Why can't people tell stories that *don't* have ghosts in them?"

I didn't have a chance to answer that question. I suddenly noticed something, and jumped to my feet.

"Maybe," I said, "we should have built this campfire *outdoors* instead of in the living room."

"Why?" Wacky Jackie asked.

"Because the house is on fire!" I cried.

THREE

"What should we do?" Babbling Brooke asked.

"*Run!*" I shouted, then spun to the door and took off.

The others leaped to their feet and came running after me. Our shoes thudded on the grass as we burst out into the cool night.

As we all huddled together in the front yard, we watched the fire. Flames shot out of the front windows, like they wanted to chase after us. The crackling fire was as loud as thunder.

Junkfood John bumped me on the shoulder. His eyes were wide, and he was breathing hard. "Adam, I have to go back in," he said.

"No way," I said. "Why?"

John pointed to the house. "I have no choice. I left two bags of Chipotle Corn-Dog Chips and a bag of Pretzel-Covered Sesame Seeds in there!"

John lowered his head like a bull about to charge, but I grabbed him by the shoulders and pulled him back. "I know it's a tragic loss," I explained to him. "But you can't go back in. Maybe your snacks will survive the fire."

"But I don't like them *toasted!*" John insisted.

"I know how badly you feel," I told John. "But some day in the future you'll get over your sadness."

We stood and watched the fire spread over the whole house. No one spoke. The roar of the flames was too loud to shout over.

Cranky Frankie stepped close to me, shaking his head. "This really burns me up," he said.

I think he was making a joke.

Or was he just being cranky?

I heard fire engine sirens in the distance. But I knew the fire trucks were already too late. The house was burning to the ground.

"We're lucky our neighbors are away," Babbling Brooke said. "And that we decided to camp out and light a fire in *their* house. Otherwise, we'd have nowhere to sleep tonight!"

Brooke always looks on the bright side.

FOUR

Hi, everyone. Brainy Janey here. I'm going to continue our exciting camp story.

A week later, we were frantically packing up. The camp bus was coming for us in an hour. But what should we bring? We were all in a total panic.

I helped Nervous Rex pack his bag, which included a pair of socks and forty cans of bug spray. "Mosquitos make me nervous," Rex said. "Once, I thought I had an *enormous* mosquito bite. But it turned out to be my head."

Last week, I gave Rex a book titled *How Not to Be Nervous*. But he doesn't like to read books because he once got a paper cut.

"I can't find my stomach medicine," Luke Puke wailed. "Has anyone seen my stomach medicine? I really need it."

"Does it actually help you?" I asked.

Luke shrugged. "I don't know. Every time I take it, I puke."

"Hey, what's that pounding noise?" Adam Bomb shouted.

We all listened. Handy Sandy had put a big wooden camp trunk in the center of the floor earlier. The pounding was coming from *inside* the trunk.

Rob Slob popped the latch and lifted the trunk lid. Handy Sandy was lying down inside the trunk.

"Thanks," she said, climbing out.

"What were you doing in there?" Rob asked.

"I was putting a lamp inside the trunk so I could see my clothes in the dark," Sandy said. "But I couldn't think of a way to keep the lid open while I was inside."

Isn't she clever?

Meanwhile, Adam Bomb crossed the room to help Cranky Frankie with his camp bag. Adam struggled and strained to lift the bag, but he finally gave up. "Too heavy," he groaned.

Frankie scowled at Adam. "Are you telling me I can't bring my bowling ball to camp?"

As Adam thought about the question, I asked Junkfood John, "Did you pack a lot of snacks for camp?"

"Not a *lot*," he said.

I looked down and saw that he had packed twelve suitcases.

"Know what I'm going to do at camp?" Wacky Jackie asked. "I'm going to start a bug collection." She reached out and pulled a few large bugs from Rob Slob's hair. "Where's my collecting jar? These will get me started."

"Hey, those are mine!" Rob Slob cried. "Give 'em back!"

Babbling Brooke skipped in front of the living room window. "I'm going to do a new cheer for Camp Lemme-Owttahere!" she announced. Then she clapped her hands, leaped into the air, and cheered:

"GIVE ME A C!
"GIVE ME AN A!
"GIVE ME AN M!
"GIVE ME ANOTHER M!
"GIVE ME A P!
"WHAT DOES THAT SPELL?
"I SAID, WHAT DOES THAT SPELL?
"CAMMP!
"WE LOVE CAMMP!
"YAAAAY, CAMMP!"

Brooke is a terrible speller. But she has a lot of enthusiasm.

She ended her cheer with a backward somersault and kicked out the living room window. Glass shattered everywhere, but she didn't seem to notice.

We started to clap. But we stopped when we heard a loud knock on the front door.

Who was it? The camp bus driver? Was it time to go?

I pulled open the front door—and gasped.

"You?" I cried. "What are *you* doing here?!"

FIVE

I stared in surprise at Patty and Peter, the Perfect twins.

The Perfects live across the street from us with their parents, Parker and Penny Perfect. The family is perfect in every way. Name anything—they're perfect at it.

Patty and Peter flashed their perfect smiles, and I could see their gleaming white perfect teeth. They wore matching white Polo shirts and dark, straight-legged jeans. Their perfect white sneakers glowed so brightly, I thought their feet were on fire.

Three guesses about how my friends and I feel about Patty and Peter Perfect. You are right. We think they are perfectly awful.

But here they were, marching into our house, sweeping back their perfect hair, and gazing around the room at us with their sparkling blue eyes.

"We are going to Camp Lemme-Owttahere, too," Peter said. He stared at the bags and suitcases scattered over the floor. "We packed last year," he said. "Just so we'd be ready."

Patty frowned at me. "Your bags don't match. How can you go to camp without matching bags?"

I just stared back at Patty. I didn't know how to answer her. And I'm the brainy one in this house.

Cranky Frankie squinted at the Perfects. "Are you *sure* you want to go on the bus with us?"

"We're not taking the bus," Patty said. "Our parents are driving Peter and me to camp because they're *perfect* parents."

"The camp bus has vinyl seats," Peter added. "And we don't like to have vinyl against our perfect skin. You know how irritating vinyl can be."

"No, no we don't," Frankie muttered.

"Are you going to be in our cabin?" Babbling Brooke asked Patty.

Patty stuck a finger down her throat and pretended to gag.

"Is that a yes or a no?" Brooke asked.

"We won't be staying in some *cabin* like you guys," Patty told her. "Peter and I are bringing our own two-room tent." She sneered at Brooke. "A cabin doesn't have enough closet space for my summer wardrobe."

"And we're bringing our own hot tub so we'll be able to unwind at the end of the day," Peter said.

Peter glanced across the room. "Can I help you take that pile of garbage off the couch?"

"That isn't a pile of garbage," Adam Bomb said. "It's Rob Slob."

Adam's face was bright red. He looked about to explode. We all hate it when Adam explodes. It's so messy.

"Sorry," Peter said. "The smell is so *gross*, I just thought—"

"We're used to it," Adam said. He then took a few steps toward the Perfect twins. "So why did you two come over here?" he demanded. "Just to insult us?"

"We came over because you are our friends and we wanted to help you," Patty said.

"We thought you could use some basic lessons in first aid," Peter added. "It's important to know first aid at camp."

"Everyone always talks about first aid," I said. "But no one ever talks about *second* aid. Why is that?"

Patty and Peter stared at me as if I didn't make any sense.

It's so hard being the smartest one in the room. I sometimes wish I was half as brainy as I am!

"Why will we need first aid?" Handy Sandy asked.

"Don't you know *anything* about camp?" Peter asked. "Things get pretty rough when everyone is battling to be Camp Champ."

Nervous Rex started to shiver. "I don't like it when things get rough," he said. "I once got into a wrestling match with a stiff pair of pajamas, and I almost lost." He shivered again.

"Camp Champ?" Adam Bomb said. "What's *that*?"

SIX

I'm Babbling Brooke. I'll take the story from here.

Patty and Peter Perfect stepped around our bags and suitcases and made their way to the armchairs against the wall.

Peter pointed to the floor. "You should pick up that chocolate bar," he said, "before it melts."

"It isn't chocolate," Cranky Frankie told him. "Our dog Pooper is only four. He isn't housebroken yet."

Patty Perfect sneered. "We trained our dog *not* to poop," she said.

Rob Slob let out a long burp. He then tapped his belly. "That's the last time I'll have lima beans for breakfast," he murmured.

"Why did you have lima beans for breakfast?" I asked him.

"Because I couldn't find the pinto beans," he said, then burped again.

"Would anyone like a snack?" Junkfood John asked. He held up a brown-and-white teddy bear.

"What's that?" I asked.

"It's awesome," John said. "It's a Cheese Bear. A plush teddy bear filled with cheddar cheese." He pushed it toward me. "Want to try a leg?"

Luke Puke made an **ULLLLLP** sound. He pressed his hand over his mouth and went running to the bathroom.

"So, tell us about Camp Champ," Adam Bomb said. "What does that mean?"

"It means the winner is champ of the camp," Peter Perfect answered.

"We're all going to play a lot of sports at camp," Patty said. "All kinds of games and sports and competitions. And everyone who wins gets points."

"Winning makes me nervous," Nervous Rex said. "Too much pressure. And winning makes me feel sad for everyone who *doesn't* win."

"When did *you* ever win anything?" Cranky Frankie asked.

"I won a staring contest once," Rex said. "I was

competing against myself in a mirror. And believe it or not, my reflection was the first to blink."

"If you don't play sports, you can't be Camp Champ," Peter said.

"You mean Camp *Chump*," Cranky Frankie muttered.

"Do you always have such a bad attitude?" Patty asked him.

"Not always," Frankie said. "Just when I'm awake."

"The camper who is the biggest winner is named Camp Champ," Patty Perfect said. "You get to boss everyone around, and eat whatever you like, and do whatever you want."

"Everyone else has to bow down to you and serve your every wish," Peter added. "It's like being an *emperor* for a whole day!"

"You get to eat *whatever you want*? Seriously?" Junkfood John said. He took a big bite of his cheese-stuffed teddy bear.

"Sounds like fun!" I said. "I'll do a cheer for the Camp Champ. Who do you think will win?"

"Well, you all can forget about winning," Patty said. "Peter and I are Camp Champs *every year*."

"One summer," Peter said, "we stayed home. We didn't even *go* to camp and we were *still* voted Camp Champs! So . . . don't start thinking you have a chance."

"You're wrong," Adam Bomb said. "This year, one of *us* will be Camp Champ."

Patty and Peter fell off their chairs and rolled around on the floor laughing their heads off. They laughed so hard, they actually had to give each other artificial respiration. Then they picked themselves up off the floor and left. I guess first aid really *is* important.

"What's so funny?" I asked. "I don't get the joke."

Rob Slob burped again. It was such a juicy burp, I could *see* it!

"There must have been something wrong with those lima beans," Rob said. "Are lima beans supposed to have green and blue lumps growing on them?"

SEVEN

Hey, it's me, Cranky Frankie. Shut your yaps and let me continue the story.

I don't want to talk about our bus ride to Camp Lemme-Owttahere. For one thing, Luke Puke got bus sick. Bet you couldn't see that coming. The bus had only gone two blocks when Luke did his thing.

It was a pretty smelly ride the rest of the way.

Babbling Brooke wanted to sing camp songs. But we don't know any camp songs because we've never been to camp.

So she stood up and did one of her cheers. She jumped up so high at the end of the cheer the driver had to stop the bus and pry Brooke's head from one of the storage racks.

She was quiet after that.

Junkfood John passed around some of his favorite snacks—bags of Malted Goat Intestine Chips and Red Hot Sushi Cheese Balls—in case anyone got hungry. I begged him not to, but Luke Puke ate a handful of Sushi Cheese Balls. And then he did his thing all over again.

I was one of the lucky ones. He didn't get any on me.

We passed by a lot of little towns and farms, and soon we were in the woods. The bus turned into a narrow dirt road, and we bumped along—not singing camp songs but covering our noses and mouths—until we reached the front gate of Camp Lemme-Owttahere.

My friends are all lame-brained good-for-nothing fatheaded moron creep faces, and I'll smack anyone who says I don't love every one of them. But, believe me, I couldn't wait to climb off that stinky bus.

And I wasn't the only one. It was a sunny day without a cloud in the sky, and the tall trees all around us shimmered like emeralds. I *hate* shimmering trees—don't you?

I was gazing at the rows of wooden cabins when Rob Slob bumped up against me with a big grin. "Hey, I won the farting contest!" he declared.

I frowned at him. "Rob, you were the only one playing. Of course you won the contest."

He is such a tough competitor, he didn't notice that the kids near him had all moved to the back of the bus.

Rob Slob loves contests. He has a trophy in his room for winning the head lice contest.

But that's another story.

The driver hauled our bags off the bus. And then he hauled Nervous Rex off the bus.

"Fresh air makes me nervous," Rex said. "I mean, what if it isn't that fresh? And who knows where the air has been? Did you ever think of that?"

None of us had ever thought of that. But we explained to Rex that his plan to stay on the bus until the end of summer probably wasn't the *best* plan.

The driver groaned and grabbed his back as he dropped my bag on the ground. You see, I didn't listen to my friends. I brought my bowling ball to camp anyway. Just in case.

What's the big deal? It's just a bowling ball.

We all turned when we heard a shout. A bouncy bald guy in an enormous red sweatshirt and white shorts was running across the grass and waving at us with both hands.

Camp was about to begin.

EIGHT

"Ricky ticky, everyone!" the man shouted, bouncing up to us. He had sweat pouring down his round face—from running, I guess—and he picked up a clipboard and grinned. "Ricky ticky to all you new Lemmes!"

I turned to Brainy Janey. "What language is he speaking?"

Janey shrugged. "Beats me. I think it's camp talk."

The man mopped beads of sweat off his bald head with his free hand. "Let's all go plummy!" he shouted. "Welcome! Welcome! Are you all as plummy as I am to be here today?"

He looked disappointed that none of us answered. But we didn't know what he was saying.

I turned back to Brainy Janey. "Are you feeling *plummy*?" I whispered.

Janey shrugged again. "I'm not sure."

30

"Ricky ticky!" the man repeated in a booming deep voice. "Booyah! Plummy days, everyone! Let's go, Lemmes!"

Babbling Brooke pumped her fists in the air. "Let's go, Lemmes!" she shouted. Brooke thinks everything is a cheer. I stared at her. I think Brooke actually understood him!

"Ricky ticky and booyah!" the man boomed. "I'm Ernie Cousin. I own this camp. Rah-rah gopher grits!"

The man's eyes moved from camper to camper. "Gopher grits?" he demanded. "Rah-rah gopher grits?"

We all muttered something in response.

"Yes, I'm the camp owner. I'm Ernie Cousin," he repeated. "But everyone here calls me Uncle Cousin!"

"He's starting to make sense," Wacky Jackie said.

Uncle Cousin let out a cheer. "Gopher grits gumbo! Go for it! Ricky ticky! Go for it!"

Nervous Rex hid behind me. "Can I get b-back on the bus?" he stammered.

I didn't have a chance to answer him. A woman came marching up to us, poking a long wooden cane in the grass as she walked. Squinting into the sun, I saw that she was also wearing a red sweatshirt and white shorts.

She was a young woman, and she had purple hair and tiny eyes. She strode up to us and pounded her cane into the grass.

And I gasped. We all gasped.

We knew her.

It was Mama—the woman Brainy Janey had hired to play our mother when we needed one a few months ago.

Mama was a disaster. And I'm not being cranky when I say that. She drove us *all* crazy. And it took everything we could think of to get rid of her.

And now here she was, stomping up in the big biker boots she always wore, dressed in the camp sweatshirt and shorts, and waving her cane at us.

Uncle Cousin slapped her on the back. "Plummy!" he declared. "Plum pudding! Booyah!"

Mama moved up to us, shaking her head and muttering under her breath.

"Ricky ticky, Lemmes!" Uncle Cousin said. "Meet our head counselor. You can call her Mama."

Mama swung her cane and slapped Adam Bomb on the back with it.

"OWWWW!" he wailed, and fell to his knees.

"I remember you, Ferret Face!" she cried. "That's a camp welcome for you!"

Mama turned to the rest of us. "I remember all you dum-diddies!"

Nervous Rex poked me in the back. "P-please bury me right here," he whispered.

I wasn't happy to see Mama, either. She swung a mean cane. And her idea of being friendly was to call us horrible names and trash everything we did.

"Welcome to camp!" she cried. "Or should I say, welcome to your worst nightmare!"

Uncle Cousin laughed. He thought she was joking. But we knew she wasn't.

Mama jammed the tip of her cane into Rob Slob's

foot, and he hopped away in pain. "Hey, cluck-cluck," she called after him. "Man up! No pain, no gain!"

Uncle Cousin nodded his sweaty, round head. "It's a long way to Tipperary!" he boomed.

"K-kill me now," Nervous Rex begged.

"You cluck-clucks are going to play your hearts out at this camp," Mama said. "Or else you'll die trying! *Hahaha*. Just messing with you. Not!"

"Plummy!" the camp owner agreed.

I promise you'll have fun—or I'll *beat* it out of you! *Hahaha*."

Mama was definitely in a good mood.

She swung her cane at Adam Bomb again, but this time she missed. She swung so hard she hit herself in the head. Dazed, she staggered back against a tree.

Uncle Cousin motioned for us to follow. "Ricky ticky, everyone!" he called. As he walked, he lowered his eyes to his clipboard. "Cabin assignments," he said. "Cabin assignments. Every Lemme in a cabin. Plummy!"

We followed the camp owner across the grass. Junkfood John and I were at the back of the line, and I turned to him and asked, "Are we having fun yet?"

He rubbed his belly. "When's lunch?"

NINE

Adam Bomb here. I think I'd better take over the story from Cranky Frankie.

Yes, I was ready to explode when I saw Mama again. And I was very unhappy that she was our head counselor. But as I followed the weird camp owner to the cabins, I started to cheer up.

Here I was with my best buddies, in the woods on the shores of beautiful Lake Bleccch. We had the whole summer ahead of us to have fun in the fresh air and play sports and hang out and swim and have campfires in the great outdoors.

What could be bad?

The boys' cabins were on one side of the lake, and the girls' cabins on the other. As we passed by, Peter and Patty Perfect waved to us from in front of their

gigantic, two-bedroom tent. They were already dressed in red and white, the camp colors.

Three workers in camp uniforms were installing their hot tub. And a pennant was flying on a flagpole beside their tent. In the bright sunlight, it was hard to read. But I think the pennants said PLUMMY.

Patty and Peter *really* wanted to be Camp Champs.

I hoped this was the year we could stop them.

We said goodbye to the girls as Uncle Cousin pointed the rest of us to Cabin Number 4. Wow. All six of us in one cabin together. Sweet!

But we had a surprise when we stepped into the cabin. We counted three bunk beds and a cot—room enough for seven. And a seventh kid—someone we'd never seen before—had already claimed one of the top bunks.

The kid turned when we piled in and we all gasped in surprise. *He looked a lot like us!*

He seemed shocked to see us, too. "Dudes," he said. "Dudes."

"Hey," I said, and flashed him a friendly smile. "How's it going, *dude*? Where are you from?"

He smiled back. "Dudes," he said again. He seemed to be stuck on that word.

"They call us the Garbage Pail Kids," Rob Slob said.

"Whoa." His eyes grew wide. "They call me a Garbage Pail Kid, too!" he exclaimed.

"Weird," I said. "Where do you come from?"

"Somewhere in that direction," he said, pointing behind him. "But I grew up over there." He pointed to his left.

"You don't know where you're from?" I asked.

He blinked. "Am I supposed to? Will I be quizzed later?"

We told him our names. Then we waited for him to tell us his.

"Pat Splat," he said.

He climbed down from the bunk bed, raised a hand, and started to cross the cabin toward us as if we were all going to do the secret Garbage Pail Kids handshake. (It's such a secret, none of us knows how to do it.)

But he tripped on a skateboard in the middle of the floor, went sailing over the cot, and slammed into one of the bunk beds. A heavy wooden camp trunk then fell on his head.

SPLLAAAAAAT.

"I think we know how he got his name," Cranky Frankie said.

TEN

Handy Sandy here to continue the story.

Head Counselor Mama led us four girls to our cabin on the other side of Lake Bleccch. Cabin Number 12. Her biker boots thudded over the grass.

"You dib-dabs have the best cabin," she said, pointing to the square log cabin with her cane. "The window doesn't close, and the floorboards are loose, and there's a few leaks in the roof. But trust me, yuk-yuks. It's the best cabin."

"Is there a bathroom?" Babbling Brooke asked.

Mama scowled at her. "A bathroom? What do you think the woods are for?"

"But—but—" Brooke started to protest.

"There's a bathroom twenty minutes away in town," Mama told her. "A shuttle bus leaves twice a day."

"Oh," Brooke said. "That's better."

We walked up to the front door, which seemed to be stuck open.

"I forgot to mention the fruit flies," Mama said.

Wacky Jackie squinted at her. "Fruit flies?"

Mama nodded. "Yes. They come with the cabin. But don't worry, you don't have to pay extra."

"The fruit flies are free?" Jackie asked.

Mama nodded again. "But we do have to charge extra for the mosquitoes."

"Makes sense," Jackie said.

"Why are there fruit flies?" I asked. "Is there fruit in the cabin?"

"There better not be, dum-dum!" Mama snapped. "No fruit allowed in the cabin!"

"I did a study on fruit flies," Brainy Janey said. "The odd thing is, they are neither fruit nor flies. They are actually legumes."

"Wowser. That is so interesting," Mama said. She then stuck two fingers down her throat and pretended to gag.

As I followed the other girls into the cabin, we all waved our hands frantically in front of us, trying to brush away the fruit flies.

When I could finally see, I counted three bunk beds in the cabin. And I recognized the girl resting in one of them—Nasty Nancy.

We had already met Nancy and her friends at the Smellville Pet Show a while back. They claimed to be Garbage Pail Kids, too. But how is that possible?

Nasty Nancy jumped up from her bunk and frowned at us.

"You again!" Babbling Brooke exclaimed. "Are you happy to see us?"

"Am I happy to get a skin rash?" Nancy replied. "Can we vote on who stays—you or the fruit flies?"

"You will never be Camp Champ with *that* attitude," I told her.

"You'll never be Camp Champ with that big red lump on your head!" Nasty Nancy replied.

"I don't have a big red lump on my head," I said.

Nancy pumped her fists. "I can give you one."

"Hey, you cluck-clucks. No violence at this camp!" Mama cried. She swung her cane and smacked Nancy in the back with it.

"Don't make me teach you lame-brain pig-faced losers a lesson," Mama said. "No violence, and no name-calling."

I heard a loud cough from the back of the cabin. "Is someone else here?" I asked.

"Meet your other bunkmate," Mama said.

I gazed around the cabin, but I couldn't see anyone. My eyes stopped at a tall mound of goo at the back wall. I blinked a few times and tried to focus. It looked like a lime-green, gooey pile of snot.

"Meet Leaky Lindsay," Mama said. She waved at the mound with her cane. "Don't be shy, you snot-rag. Come over here."

The pile of thick goo slid toward us, and I could see her more clearly. Leaky Lindsay was leaking wet snot from her nose *and* her mouth. It even seemed to be coming out of her ears! And her brown hair was drenched.

Her T-shirt and shorts were caked with snot, which dripped down to her sneakers.

"Does anyone have a tissue?" she asked. "I forgot to bring any."

"You poor thing," Babbling Brooke said. "Do you have a cold?"

"No," she replied.

Mama checked the big watch on her wrist. "I'll let you dim-dums unpack," she said. "But you'd better hurry. We have an important camp meeting in thirty seconds."

ELEVEN

Adam Bomb here again. You're going to **E-X-P-L-O-D-E** when you read what happened next.

We all gathered for our first camp meeting. We were headed to a circle of low benches between the mess hall and the activities building.

As we walked over to join the others, we passed the supply cabin and the equipment shack. And we were almost to the meeting grounds when Pat Splat tripped over a fallen tree branch and smashed his head against the flagpole.

SPLAAAAAAT.

We helped Pat to his feet and he walked in zigzags the rest of the way. But he swore he was okay.

I thought I heard some kind of wild animal growling behind us in the woods, but it was just Junkfood John's stomach. It was noon, and we hadn't had any lunch yet.

The girls were already at the meeting grounds. So we guys found seats on the lower benches. Everyone except Nervous Rex.

Rex refused to leave the cabin—we left him hiding under his bunk. "Call me in September," he said.

I pleaded with him to come to the meeting. "Rex, you'll never be Camp Champ if you don't come out from under the bed."

"I want to be *Cabin* Champ," he said.

I didn't have the heart to tell him I'd already seen a mouse in our cabin. I didn't want to spoil his day.

There were at least thirty campers at the meeting. Most of them were strangers. I saw Babbling Brooke sitting with someone I didn't recognize. The girl kept wiping thick goo from her nose and mouth. I think she was using a bath towel for a tissue.

And I saw Nasty Nancy, a girl we met at the Smellville Pet Show last fall. I waved to her, and she stuck her tongue out and made a very rude noise with it. She really is nasty.

The round, red-faced camp owner, Uncle Cousin, stepped into the middle of the circle. A man in an apron and wearing a tall, white chef's cap stood next to him.

"Plum pudding, everyone!" Uncle Cousin exclaimed. "Plummy, all! Booyah!"

He waited for us to respond. But, of course, no one knew how.

"Our camp chef," Cousin said. He put a hand on the man's shoulder. "Chef Indy. Let me introduce Chef Indy Jestian."

Chef Indy smiled and nodded, and his chef's cap fell into the dirt. It took him a while to dust it off and get it back on his head.

"Ricky ticky! Chef Indy makes a chipmunk salad

to die for!" Uncle Cousin exclaimed. "You will all be enjoying it soon."

"YAAAAY!" Babbling Brooke jumped to her feet and cheered.

Brooke cheers at anything. She even cheers at toenail clippings.

"Chipmunks have been scarce this year," Uncle Cousin continued. "But we think we will almost have enough to go around."

"YAAAAY." Brooke cheered again. Then she saw she was the only one cheering for chipmunk salad, so she dropped back onto her bench.

"I have a special announcement," Chef Indy said. A gust of wind came up, and his chef's cap blew off his head and sailed over the meeting grounds.

"I'll get it!" Pat Splat cried. He took off after the cap. But he tripped over a bench and smashed his head against one of the concrete planters.

SPLAAAAAT.

The cap sailed over the mess hall and out of sight. Pat Splat crawled back to the bench on his hands and knees. "It got away," he mumbled.

Chef Indy's long black hair waved in the breeze. "I am

going to announce the first camp activity," he shouted. "It's a very special activity for all you Lemmes. I call it Catch Your Own Dinner."

We all leaned forward to hear better. We weren't sure we'd heard him correctly.

"It's called Catch Your Own Dinner," Indy repeated. "You see, the food truck hasn't arrived, and there's no food!"

TWELVE

"Rah! Rah! Booyah! That's the spirit!" Uncle Cousin exclaimed. "Everyone into the woods. A Lemme never says the word *starvation!*"

We all looked at one another.

"Ricky ticky! Rah! Rah!" Uncle Cousin boomed. "A hunting we will go. We won't stop until there's food for almost everyone! Booyah!"

I took a deep breath. I had an empty feeling in my stomach. Mainly because my stomach was empty!

Across the meeting grounds, Peter and Patty Perfect jumped to their feet. "No problem!" Peter declared. "Patty and I are champs at feeding ourselves."

They darted over to a low tree. "We've been studying up on edible tree leaves," Patty said.

"That's right," Peter said. "Tree leaves are one of our favorite food groups. We'll just make a nice salad."

They began pulling the leaves off the tree and shoving them into their mouths.

"You can't be Camp Champ if you don't know how to feed yourself," Patty said. Some green leaf juice ran down her chin. She burped. It was a perfect burp, just long enough not to be gross.

Chewing hard, Peter held up a leaf with a big white blob on it. "Bird poop is the perfect salad dressing!" He gobbled it up, but it didn't seem like he really liked it.

Luke Puke made an **ULLLLP** sound. He covered his mouth and ran behind the mess hall to puke his guts out.

I thought about Nervous Rex, who was hiding in the cabin. How nervous will Rex get when he finds out we have to hunt for our own dinner?

Junkfood John bumped my shoulder. "Hey, Adam," he said. "I packed three suitcases of chips and salsa. Think that will be enough?"

"Enough to share?" I said.

He shook his head. "No, enough for *me*."

Suddenly, Nasty Nancy jumped to her feet and let out a shrill scream. We all jumped to our feet.

Her eyes were wide with fright, and she pointed to the woods. "Bear!" she screamed. "Look! A bear! There's a bear in the camp!"

Terrified screams broke out as the creature lumbered toward us.

"Wait, everyone!" I cried, waving my hands above my head. "Hold on. That's just Rob Slob."

"He really needs a bath," Cranky Frankie said.

The meeting was over, and we all headed back to our cabins to get ready for our food hunt in the woods. Wacky Jackie walked up beside me. "Do you know how to set a trap for a hamburger and french fries?" she asked.

Was she joking? I wasn't so sure.

"I heard there are pizza trees in the woods," I told her. "When you harvest them, you just have to be careful the cheese doesn't slide off."

She nodded. I think she may have believed me.

We split up, and I followed the other guys to Cabin 4.

Nervous Rex came out from under his bunk when we came in. "Is it lunch time?" he asked.

"Not quite," I said. "We have to go into the woods and find our *own* lunch. We came back here first to get ready."

"Hunting for food makes me nervous," Rex said. "And the woods make me nervous. All those trees. What if one of them falls on us?"

"I hate when that happens," Pat Splat said. "A tree fell on my head last spring, and it almost ruined my day."

Junkfood John sat on a bunk in the corner. He had a bag of chips tilted over his face and was letting them pour into his open mouth.

"I hear mushrooms are good to eat," I said.

Nervous Rex gasped. "Well, be careful not to pick any of the poisonous mushrooms," he said.

Cranky Frankie squinted at him. "Rex," he said, "how do we know which ones are poisonous?"

"I guess you find out after you eat them," Rex said.

BRAINY JANEY'S WILDERNESS SURVIVAL QUIZ

Here is a quiz for anyone who goes into the woods and wants to come back. How many can you get right? You'll find the answers after the quiz. No peeking!

QUESTIONS

1. If you get lost, you can always tell which direction is north by
   _____.

2. You can survive a cold night by making a fire. Just take two
   sticks and _____.

3. The easiest way to identify a poison ivy leaf is by _____.

4. True or False?

5. If you don't have insect spray, the best way to avoid insects is
   to _____.

6. Raccoons won't bite you if _____.

7. True or False: A large brown bear in the woods is just as afraid
   of *you* as you are of it.

8. In deep woods at night, the best way to avoid getting cold is
   to _____.

9. To avoid getting wet in a rainstorm, you should _____.

10. Bonus Question: What is a bonus?

ANSWERS

1. asking someone.

2. light them with a match.

3. rubbing it on your face.

4. False.

5. stay indoors.

6. you don't bite them.

7. Don't be ridiculous.

8. zip up your jacket.

9. run between the raindrops.

10. Beats me!

THIRTEEN

Babbling Brooke here. Yea! I get to continue our story now.

"AHHH-CHOOO!"

Leaky Lindsay sneezed for the tenth time in a row.

"AHHH-CHOOO!"

Make that eleven. Then she used the blanket off her bed as a tissue.

"Are you sure you don't have a cold?" Nasty Nancy asked her.

"I feel fine," Lindsay replied, mopping thick globs of snot from her hair. "I think it's just allergies."

Nasty Nancy moved to the other side of the cabin. "I'm allergic to *you*!" she told Lindsay.

The rest of us were excited to be going into the woods to hunt for our dinner. I was so excited, I performed a cheer that I made up on the spot.

"GIVE ME AN F!
"GIVE ME A U!
"GIVE ME A D!
"GIVE ME AN E!
"WHAT DOES THAT SPELL?
"FUDE!
"FUDE, FUDE, FUDE!
"I LIKE TO EAT FUDE!"

I jumped high and smashed my head into one of the wooden cabin rafters. After a few minutes, it only hurt a little bit.

What *did* hurt was that the other girls just stood and stared at me and didn't join in my cheer.

"Aren't you excited about going on the hunt?" I asked. "Going into the wilderness on our own?"

"It's about as exciting as diaper rash," Nasty Nancy said.

I didn't get what she meant.

"Maybe we should start at the lake," Wacky Jackie said.

Brainy Janey squinted at her. "Why the lake?"

"We could get a big net and see what we can bring up," Jackie said. "I'm *dying* for a tuna fish sandwich!"

"I don't think there are any tuna fish sandwiches in Lake Bleccch," Handy Sandy said.

Nasty Nancy scowled at Wacky Jackie. "Did anyone ever tell you you're an awesome brainiac?"

Jackie shook her head. "No," she said. "No one ever said that to me. But thank you."

Nancy rolled her eyes. "Wonder why," she muttered.

Wacky Jackie ignored her. "Maybe we could find fish sticks," she said. "I love fish sticks."

"I don't think so," Brainy Janey said. "Fish sticks can only be found in saltwater, and this is a freshwater lake." Janey chuckled. "The funny thing about fish sticks is that they're not fish and they're not sticks. They are actually a *legume*."

Nasty Nancy shook her head. "That's so interesting," she said sarcastically. "Remind me to write home to Mom and Dad and tell them. Oh, right. We don't have parents."

Brainy Janey stamped her foot. "Nancy, don't you ever get tired of being nasty?"

"Me? Nasty?" Nancy replied. "I don't have a nasty bone in my body. And I'll smack you if you say I'm nasty!"

"AHHHHH-CHOOO."

Leaky Lindsay forgot to cover her nose, and for a moment, I thought it was raining inside the cabin.

"Let me show you what I built," Handy Sandy said. She reached under her bunk and pulled something out.

It was a metal contraption, and it looked like a sawblade bent to fit a wide metal ring.

"What's that?" Wacky Jackie asked. "Your dental retainer?"

"No," Sandy said. "I built an animal trap." She held it up in both hands. "See? We hide this on the ground under some leaves. And when an animal comes along— **SNAP!** We have our dinner."

"It looks dangerous," I said. "Are you sure it's safe?"

"Of course," Sandy said. "You know how skillful I am. Would I build a trap that isn't safe?"

I studied the metal contraption. The blade had dozens of pointy teeth and was coiled tightly on the base.

"I'll show you how to arm the trap," Handy Sandy said. "Watch this. It's easy. Even a child could do it."

She held the base in one hand and pulled the sawblade up in the other.

SNAAAAAAAAAAPPPPP!

Handy Sandy let out a shrill howl of pain and did a crazy panic dance, waving her hand in the air with the trap snapped over her arm. *"Helllllllp meeeee!"*

"I think it needs more work," Nasty Nancy said.

We helped Sandy remove the trap from her arm.

"You might be right," she said. "I think it needs a little less zing in the spring."

"Let's get going, girls!" I cried. "Rah-rah! Booyah! Last one into the woods is a rotten Lemme!"

So we burst out of the cabin into the afternoon sunlight and hurried toward the tangled trees that surrounded the camp.

And did we have a big surprise waiting for us in the woods? I'll give you three guesses!

FOURTEEN

Sunlight flickered down through the treetops. The ground was covered in a soft blanket of dead leaves from last fall. Our shoes crunched over twigs and tall grass.

I felt so excited to be here in the woods with my friends. Every shimmering leaf and billowy reed waving in the wind made me hope we would have great success on our food hunt.

Brainy Janey led the way, and we followed in a single line. The path was very narrow.

She suddenly stopped and pointed at a row of low shrubs. "Those berries look good enough to eat," she said.

Wacky Jackie plucked a few of the red berries off the bush and shoved them into her mouth. "Yes. Very sweet," she said, swallowing loudly.

As berry juice ran down Jackie's chin, she plucked another handful and swallowed them.

"I believe they are wild mooseberries," Janey said, examining a few in her hand. "Mooseberries are very rare. In fact, they are extinct. So it's lucky we found some."

"About as lucky as diaper rash," Nasty Nancy said.

What was her *problem* with diaper rash?

"We need to bring back a lot of these berries," Brainy Janey said. "Did anyone bring a basket for carrying things?"

Silence. We all shook our heads.

"Did anyone bring a cup or a bowl?" Janey asked.

No. No one.

"Does anyone have a backpack we could put them in?" Janey asked.

We glanced around and looked at one another. No. No backpacks.

"Does anyone have any pockets?" Janey asked.

We all checked our shorts.

No. No pockets.

"We could cup our hands and carry them back," Wacky Jackie said.

"If our hands are filled with berries, how can we hunt for other food?" Handy Sandy asked.

Wacky Jackie made a loud **URRRRRP** sound. Her mouth dropped open and she moaned. *"Ohhhh. I don't feel so good."* She gripped her stomach. *"Maybe those berries . . ."* Her voice trailed off and she **URRRRRPED** again.

"I *knew* those berries were bad. Let's forget the berries," Brainy Janey said. "We need to find some *real* food."

We moved on, following the trail. We had to step over a fallen tree branch, and kick a stack of dead weeds out of our way.

I heard the flutter of birds in the trees above us. And somewhere in the far distance, an animal howled.

We stopped at the edge of a small clearing. "Check that out," Handy Sandy said, pointing to something in the grass.

We all stepped closer to see what it was.

"It's a bone," Sandy said. "Some kind of animal bone."

She was right. We studied it in silence.

"This is good," Sandy said, turning to us. "Because where there's bones, there's got to be meat."

FIFTEEN

I know I get excited easily. But now I was *really* pumped. We were on the trail of meat! My mouth was watering just thinking about it.

"Chef Indy will think we're awesome," I said. "And I know we'll get points in the Camp Champ competition."

My heart was pounding as we roamed off the trail. I wanted to burst into song or do a cheer, but that would probably scare the meat away.

We walked in tall weeds for a few minutes—and found another bone.

"We're going the right way," Brainy Janey said, and brushed away a buzzing swarm of gnats. "Keep going, girls. This is getting *real*."

We walked on.

A few minutes later, we saw a dog.

He was tall and dark brown, lumbering noisily between the trees.

"What is that dog doing way out here?" Wacky Jackie asked.

Brainy Janey raised a finger to her lips. "Shhhh. We don't want the dog to know we're following it," she whispered.

The trees were thick overhead, and there was little sunlight. The dog walked slowly, steadily through the shadows. His head bobbed up and down as he clumped forward. And his paws crunched heavily over twigs and dry leaves.

We followed on tiptoes, trying to be as silent as we could.

Was the dog leading us to our dinner?

My eyes went wide as I saw a tall mound of rocks up ahead. Squinting in the shadowy light, I could see a low cave cut into the rocks. The dog picked up speed as it headed to the cave.

We followed close behind. But then, the dog turned around.

Did it see us?

"Whoa." Brainy Janey stopped short. Wacky Jackie bumped into her from behind. "What's up?" Jackie asked. "Why did you stop?"

Janey turned to us. "It . . . it isn't a dog," she stammered. "I read a bunch of wildlife guides before we came here. That isn't a dog."

"Then what is it?" I demanded.

"It's a bear."

I let out a loud gasp. "We've been following a *bear*?!" I cried.

Janey raised her finger to her lips again. "Shhhh," she hissed. "Listen to me. The bear won't bother you unless you show fear."

Janey paused for a moment, then added, "But I could be wrong about that."

There was only one thing to do. Make that two:

We all (1) screamed and (2) ran for our lives.

SIXTEEN

I'm Wacky Jackie, and I'll continue this horror story.

Sure, we all ran for our lives. But it seemed like the right thing to do with a large brown bear lumbering after us.

I heard a long, loud growl behind me that didn't sound at all friendly. As I ran over the dead leaves and fallen twigs and low shrubs, I knew what the bear was thinking. He was thinking *we* were meat!

We had been totally silent as we tracked the bear. But now, with him tracking *us*, we were all screaming our heads off. He growled and howled, and *we* screamed.

Even Brainy Janey, who is so smart she can tell a bear from a dog, was shrieking and wailing as she ran toward the camp. And Nasty Nancy kept turning back and yelling at the bear, "Go home! Go home!"

But I don't think it understood English, because it followed us right into camp.

Patty and Peter Perfect waved to us from their tent as we ran screaming by. Adam Bomb and Junkfood John saw us coming and ducked behind a cabin.

I ran to the mess hall. My idea was to burst inside and shut the doors behind me. But I wasn't fast enough.

I stumbled on the wooden stairs. And when I turned around, the bear had me trapped against the wall.

It let out a victory roar and stood up on its hind legs, snarling and drooling hungrily. Its shadow washed over me, and then it raised itself high and started to wrap its heavy paws around me.

I screamed.

The bear's eyes went wide. And to my surprise, it lifted its paws and took a step back.

The bear tilted his head from side to side, as if he were confused. He retreated another step. Then he raised his snout and sniffed the air noisily.

SNIFF SNIFF SNIFFFFF.

I stood frozen against the wall, too frightened to move.

The bear did some more sniffing. And then he curled

his lips and made a whimpering sound. I swear he had a sick look on his face.

What was going on?

I turned and saw Rob Slob standing nearby.

The bear whimpered like a hurt puppy. He sniffed again and took another step back.

It took me a few seconds to realize that Rob Slob was a hero.

The bear couldn't stand Rob's smell!

The bear raised his head to the sky and let out a long howl. Then he dropped to all fours, turned, and went galloping off to the woods.

"What's up?" Rob Slob asked me.

I said, "Rob, whatever you do, don't take a bath this summer."

"I won't," he replied. "Actually, I don't remember how."

SEVENTEEN

Adam Bomb here. I was getting ready to go into the woods with the other guys and hunt for our dinner, so I'll continue the story.

Everyone was set to go, except for Nervous Rex. He said he'd wait for us in the cabin, and he wished us all good luck.

We passed around a can of bug spray, and we sprayed it over our faces, hands, arms, and legs. Then Cranky Frankie looked at the can and groaned. "This isn't bug spray," he said. "It's Liquid Grease."

I took the can from him and read the label. He was right. We had sprayed ourselves with cooking grease.

"Why do we have a spray can of grease in the cabin?" I asked.

No one answered. But then Junkfood John raised

his hand. "I brought a couple of cans," he confessed. "It isn't bad if you get really thirsty."

"John, why don't you just drink water instead?" Luke Puke asked.

Junkfood John rubbed his jaw. "Water. Oh yeah. Water. I didn't think of that."

Luke Puke made a disgusted face. "Now we all smell like cooking grease. Hope it doesn't make me puke."

Cranky Frankie rolled his eyes. "Waking up in the morning makes you puke," he said.

We stepped out into the sunlight. It was a beautiful day, and the sun felt warm on my face as it started to heat up the cooking grease. The girls' cabins were empty, which meant they must already be in the woods.

A skinny gray squirrel darted past us. "Catch it!" Rob Slob cried. "We can skin it and roast it over the campfire."

Luke Puke grabbed his stomach. **"ULLLP.** First chipmunk salad. Now *squirrels*?"

Junkfood John smiled. "I had squirrel-on-a-stick once at a carnival," he said.

"What did it taste like?" Luke Puke asked him.

John shrugged. "It was okay, but the stick was better."

As we walked into the woods, Junkfood John continued. "I once had fish sticks on a stick."

"What did it taste like?" I asked.

"Chicken," he said. He turned to me. "Do you notice that everything always tastes like chicken? No matter what you cook, it tastes exactly like chicken."

"That's deep," Cranky Frankie said.

"Duck!" Luke Puke said.

"Yes. Duck can be very tasty," Junkfood John said.

"No, duck!" Luke Puke cried.

"In fact, I even had duck-on-a-stick once," Junkfood John said.

"NOOO!" Luke Puke screamed, pointing. "Duck! Duck!"

I heard a loud **CRAACK** overhead and looked up in time to see a big branch break off a tree and come crashing down.

It landed on top of Pat Splat.

He hit the ground and didn't get up.

"Funny," Junkfood John said, "duck-on-a-stick tastes a lot like chicken, too."

EIGHTEEN

It took a long time to revive Pat Splat.

I thought maybe he'd wake up if we tickled him.

Luke Puke thought we should give him mouth-to-mouth resuscitation, but no one wanted to do that.

"Maybe we should pull the tree branch off him first," Cranky Frankie suggested.

We tugged the branch away and, sure enough, Pat sat up and seemed to be okay. Well . . . almost okay.

"Is my head on backward?" he asked.

I nodded. "Yeah," I said. "But it will probably turn back around."

"You can always just put your clothes on backward," Rob Slob said.

"Isn't that furry green shirt of yours on backward?" I asked Rob Slob.

"I'm still not wearing a shirt," Rob said.

He's the only dude I know who looks good in mold.

I gazed up, and my eye caught something in another tree branch. "Hey, guys, check it out," I said pointing.

They all followed my gaze. "Is that a bird's nest?" Junkfood John asked.

I nodded. "Yes, it's a nest. A very *big* bird's nest. Maybe there are eggs in there. Then Chef Indy can make us an omelet!"

My stomach growled. I was hungrier than I thought. I imagined a big, tasty omelet on my plate with potatoes and bacon. "Who wants to climb up and check it out?" I asked.

No one volunteered.

"Tree bark makes me nauseous," Luke Puke said, holding his stomach.

"You have to get over that problem, Luke," I said. "We're going to be spending a lot of time this summer in the woods. Now go on. This will be good for you." I gave him a push toward the tree.

"I . . . don't . . . think . . . so," Luke said.

I gave him another push. Then I took his hands and wrapped them around the tree trunk. "Go ahead. Climb up and see what's in the nest. You want to be Camp Champ—don't you?"

I didn't give him a chance to answer. I gave Luke a hard boost to get him started up the tree.

The other guys all clapped. "Go, Luke! Go, Luke!"

I wished Babbling Brooke was here. She could do a cheer to encourage him to climb. It would probably go something like this . . .

"GO, LUKE!

"GO, LUKE!

"LUKE, DON'T PUKE!"

Maybe I should write cheers, too.

We all stood around the tree and watched as Luke climbed the trunk. He scrabbled up in a total panic. He was so frantic, his sneakers kicked sheets of bark off the tree. We had to back away to keep from getting hit.

Finally, Luke made it up to the limb that held the bird's nest. Gripping the limb with both hands, he raised himself over the nest and peered down into it.

"I see eggs!" he shouted down. "But they're moving!"

"Huh?" I wasn't sure I heard him correctly. I cupped my hands around my mouth and shouted. "What do you mean, the eggs are moving?"

"They're walking around the nest," Luke reported. "I guess you wouldn't call them eggs. They're chicks. Baby birds."

Beside me, Junkfood John started to drool. "Baby birds. Yum."

"Come on down," I shouted to Luke. "Leave them alone and—"

I stopped because I saw a big shadow in the sky. The shadow grew larger as it flew nearer. And when it came into focus, I recognized it—a huge eagle.

"Hey, Luke—" I shouted. But I knew he couldn't hear me because the eagle was squawking and screaming too loud.

The big bird raised its wings and dove down to the nest. And then it made a horrible racket as it angrily shrieked at Luke, smacking him with its wide wings.

SMACK SMACK SMACKSMACKSMACK!

"It's the mama eagle!" Pat Splat cried. "Guess she doesn't like Luke checking out her babies."

"You think? Look out, Luke!" I cried.

The nest fell from the tree limb and landed on Pat Splat's head. He fell to the ground, but shrugged it off and got right back up. He sure is impressive in that regard.

Above our heads, the eagle was bleating like an angry goat and tearing at Luke's T-shirt with her talons.

"Oh noooo," I moaned.

The eagle dug her talons into Luke's shoulders,

flapped her wings, lifted him off the tree—and flew away with him.

We could still hear Luke's cries when he was a tiny speck in the distance.

We stood there in silence for a while, looking up at the sky. And then Junkfood John turned to me. "I wonder what eagle tastes like?" he asked.

Already a mile away, the high-flying eagle flapped its wide wings and probably wondered a similar question: *What does this kid taste like?*

NINETEEN

Brainy Janey here. I'm going to use my enormous brain to figure out how we girls can find some food in the woods. We were all disappointed that we didn't find any meat. But I knew we could do better.

We were huddled in our cabin, sitting cross-legged on the floor, sharing our ideas. Leaky Lindsay was against the wall, using her blanket for a tissue.

"I read in a magazine that there are several types of edible rocks," I told them. "The only problem is, you have to leave them in hot water for a long time to soften them up. Otherwise, you'll break your teeth."

Nasty Nancy frowned at me. "Do they really call you *Brainy* Janey?" she said with a sneer.

"I don't like to brag," I said. "But I'm the smartest student at Smellville Middle School."

"I believe it," Nasty Nancy replied.

What did she mean by that?

"I don't like to brag," I continued, "but I'm so smart, I can spell my name backward and forward and inside-out."

Nasty Nancy rolled her eyes. "Wow. Remind me to be impressed."

"I have a new animal trap," Handy Sandy said. "I know this one will work. It's big enough to trap a deer." She held up a large metal contraption shaped like a bow from a bow and arrow.

I studied the trap. "It sure looks dangerous, Sandy," I said. "How do you know it won't snap while you are holding it, like your last one did?"

"I solved that problem," Handy Sandy said. She held up the trap and pointed to a little metal lock on the side. "See? I put a safety catch on this one. It can't snap shut unless I spring the catch. Like this."

SSSNNNAAAAAAAAAAP

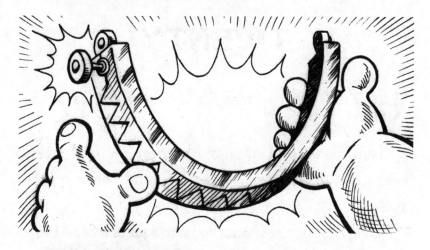

"YOWWWWWWWW!" Sandy let out a cry that could be heard across the lake. She grabbed her arm and pulled the trap off, then hopped around the cabin, screaming.

That was pretty much all we heard until Leaky Lindsay let out a loud, wet sneeze. And then another. And another.

I turned to her. "Have a cold?"

"No thanks," she said. "I think I already have one."

TWENTY

We decided to look for nuts and berries in the woods.

"How do we find nuts and berries?" Wacky Jackie asked me. She knows I've read several books on the subject.

"Well, to start, most nuts come in a jar or a can," I told her. "But you can sometimes find them in the wild."

"We should look for squirrels," Jackie said. "Because squirrels always know where to find the best nuts."

"If we were at a ball game, we could find peanuts easily," Babbling Brooke said.

"Yea, but remember, we're not at a ball game," I said. "We're in the woods."

"I love peanuts," Brooke said. "There's just one thing I don't understand. How do they get the nuts inside those little shells?

"You're *both* nuts," Nasty Nancy said. "Don't you know that nuts grow on trees? And I don't see any nut trees here in these woods."

"Nuts are actually roots," I explained to her. "You have to dig them up from the bottom of the tree." If you read as many books as I do, you'd be an expert, too.

"I'd love a big, juicy hamburger," Wacky Jackie said. "Is hamburger a fruit or a vegetable?"

"Hamburger is actually a legume," I said. "I think—"

I stopped. My eyes landed on something on the ground.

Berries.

I pointed. "Let's check out these dark berries," I said. "They look delicious."

Handy Sandy picked up a bunch of the little round berries and examined them. "These are awesome," she said. "I'll bet Chef Indy can bake us a berry pie."

My stomach was rumbling and grumbling. I pictured a warm berry pie, and it brought a smile to my face.

"I brought a basket this time," Handy Sandy said. "Let's fill it up with these berries."

And that's exactly what we did. We plucked at least a hundred berries off the ground and piled them into the basket.

"Mission accomplished!" Babbling Brooke cried.

We proudly carried them back to camp. When we found Chef Indy in the mess hall, we handed him the basket of berries.

"Look what we found!" Brooke gushed. "Awesome?"

Chef Indy gazed at the berries for a long while. Then he brought the basket close to his face and sniffed them. Then he gazed at the berries some more. Then he sniffed them again.

Then he turned to us. "Why did you bring me a basket of rabbit poop?" he asked.

TWENTY-ONE

Well, that was a major fail.

I guess it was partly my fault. I've read many books about nuts and berries. But I haven't read any books about rabbit poop.

We were all very disappointed—and hungry.

I noticed Leaky Lindsay was eating tissues one by one from a pack she had found. And Wacky Jackie had eaten the buttons off her tennis shorts.

"The boys haven't come back yet," Chef Indy said. "Maybe they will have better luck."

I went outside to wait for them, and the others followed. We all sat down on the steps of the mess hall.

While we were waiting, Patty and Peter Perfect strolled by. They were carrying bowls of tree leaves in their hands and eating them as they walked.

"How can you stand to eat tree leaves?" I asked.

"We brought our own salad dressing from home," Patty replied. "It's a strawberry vinaigrette. Organic, of course."

"It's sweet and tangy without being cloying," Peter Perfect said. "Makes a perfect salad. You should try it." He then shoved a couple more leaves into his mouth.

"We may *have* to try it," Nasty Nancy muttered.

"I ground up some birch tree bark and sprinkled it over the salad," Patty added. "It gives it such a nice birch flavor."

My stomach growled. "We're not hungry enough to eat that," I said. "But we're pretty hungry."

"We're hoping the boys will bring back something good from the woods," Handy Sandy said.

And just as she said that, I heard shouts and cheers. The boys appeared at the edge of the woods and were striding into camp.

Uncle Cousin came out of the mess hall and stepped up beside us girls on the steps. "Rah-rah! Booyah!" he cried. "Looks like we won't have to starve after all!"

Adam Bomb led the way, and he had a big smile on his face. As he and the other boys came closer, we could see that they were carrying something at their sides.

Shopping bags!

Uncle Cousin stepped forward to greet them. "Ricky ticky! What did you guys trap in the woods?" He asked.

Adam Bomb reached into a shopping bag and pulled out a package. "We found lamb chops!" he exclaimed.

Uncle Cousin's eyes went wide. He stared as Adam pulled out more packages. "Lamb chops?" Cousin said. "You butchered a *sheep*?"

"No way," Adam replied. "We found a supermarket on the highway just past the woods. They were all out of deer chops."

"We got hot dogs, too—with sauerkraut!" Junkfood John exclaimed. "And a bunch of frozen pizzas."

"YAAAAAY!" We girls jumped up and cheered.

And of course Babbling Brooke broke into a cheer . . .

"GIVE ME AN S!

"GIVE ME A U!

"GIVE ME AN I-DON'T-KNOW-

WHAT!

"HOW DO YOU SPELL

SUPERMARKET?

"I DON'T CARE!

"DON'T MAKE ME SPELL IT.

"LET'S EAT! YAAAAY!"

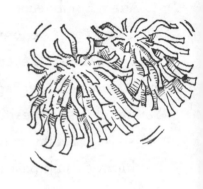

Brooke did a double cartwheel and landed facedown in the dirt.

It was maybe the worst cheer in history. It didn't even rhyme. But we helped Brooke to her feet and brushed her off.

We were all so happy we wouldn't starve.

"Uh . . . One more thing," Adam Bomb told Uncle Cousin. "Something bad happened."

The camp owner squinted at Adam. "Bad? How bad?"

Adam nodded. "Well, an eagle picked up Luke Puke and flew off with him."

Uncle Cousin slapped his own forehead. "Oh, wow," he said. "I meant to warn you about eagles." He motioned us to the mess hall door. "Well, there's not much we can do now. Might as well bring the food to Chef Indy. There's more for all of us. Let's *eat!*"

Before we could step into the mess hall, I saw something in the sky. A black speck, and it was moving toward us.

I pointed. "Look, everyone!"

The speck flew closer and I could see what it was.

An eagle.

It swooped lower, and its shadow rolled across the

ground. Then it raised its wings—and dropped Luke Puke.

"WHOOOOA!" we all shouted as Luke came falling down.

Luke fell fast—screaming all the way and flapping his arms frantically as if he could fly or slow his fall.

SPLAAAAAAT.

Luke landed on top of Pat Splat, who saved his life.

We all cheered. And were happy to see Luke again.

"What did I miss?" he asked. Then he leaned over and did his thing. If Luke were a superhero, puking would be his superpower.

Pat Splat was very flat. Adam Bomb and Rob Slob volunteered to carry him to the medical cabin. The nurse wasn't there, so they slid Pat under the door and left a note. Then we all went in to eat.

After lunch, Wacky Jackie set her laptop up on a table in the corner. She and Junkfood John sat down in front of it, and the rest of us gathered around.

Jackie had downloaded some episodes of their favorite TV show.

Jonny Pantsfalldown.

With his Pants of Steel, Jonny Pantsfalldown fights criminals courageously. His only problem as a superhero? You might be able to guess it from his name.

Jackie clicked on an episode, and we all huddled close to watch.

JONNY PANTSFALLDOWN

Favorite TV superhero of Wacky Jackie and Junkfood John
Episode 457

old on to your pants, everyone! And keep your belt buckled tight for adventure! It's time for another action-packed thriller featuring Jonny Pantsfalldown, told by me, the World's Greatest Sidekick—THE MIGHTY HAIRBALL!

"I will never let you—or my pants—down."

That's what Jonny Pantsfalldown promised the good people of Pupick Falls. And he always tries to keep most of his promises.

Every night, after a healthy dinner of fish parts and broccoli tips, Jonny puts on his cape, his mask, and his world-famous Pants of Steel. Then, side by side with me—the Mighty Hairball—he ventures out to fight crime with his bold battle cry:

"YODEL-AY-EEE-OOOO!"

Tonight, Jonny was nearly dressed when I entered his private three-room dressing pit. "Looking good, Jonny," I greeted him. "But if I may make one suggestion . . ."

Jonny turned to me with his bold X-ray eyes and X-ray nose. "Yes?"

I pointed to his snug-fitting costume. "The cape should go on the back—not the front," I told him.

"No wonder I keep falling on my face!" the great superhero exclaimed. "Hairball, where would I be without you?"

"All good sidekicks go to fashion school," I said. "That's how I know where your cape should go."

I helped Jonny tug his cape around to the back. He choked a little (sometimes he ties it a little too tight).

"Are you ready?" he boomed. Jonny has a powerful, deep voice—like thunder. Sometimes it makes your ears bleed.

"Just about," I replied. "I'm having a bit of a problem pulling on my new ostrich-feather gloves."

"Are they too tight?" Jonny asked.

I shook my head. "No. That's not the problem. You know that I have two left hands. Sometimes it makes it hard to get my gloves on."

"A hand in the bush is worth two in the gloves," Jonny said.

I didn't understand what he meant (sometimes Jonny is just too smart for me).

He straightened his Pants of Steel. "Hairball, did you bring the thumb tacks I asked you for?"

I mopped the blood from my ears with the back of my glove. "Thumb tacks?"

Jonny frowned at me. "Yes, thumb tacks. I was going to pin my Pants of Steel to my body so they don't fall down anymore."

"Sorry, Jonny. I forgot them," I said. "I may be the greatest sidekick in history, but I guess I'm not perfect."

"You can say *that* again!"

So I did. "I may be the greatest sidekick in history, but I guess I'm not perfect."

Jonny grumbled under his breath. "I didn't really *mean* for you to say it again," he muttered.

"Say it again?" I asked. "I may be the greatest sidekick in history, but I guess I'm not perfect."

Jonny gritted his teeth. "No, *please* don't say it again!" he cried.

"Again?" I said. "I may be the greatest sidekick in history, but I guess I'm not perfect."

Jonny scowled at me. "Hairball, when was the last time you had your ears examined?" he asked.

"Deer salmon?" I replied.

Jonny shook his fists in the air.

Then I realized why I couldn't hear him. I had my fur-lined, six-inch-thick brass helmet down over my ears.

I started to pull, but I couldn't get it to slide off my head. I was trapped inside my own helmet.

Maybe I can use a can opener later, I thought. Or maybe I can get the Pupick Falls fire department and they can help pull my helmet off.

In the meantime, Jonny and I had crime to fight.

"What criminal are we chasing tonight?" I asked.

"Tonight, we will be bringing down the Silver Swine," Jonny said.

"The Silver Swine?" I said. "He sounds dangerous."

"Danger is my middle name!" Jonny boomed.

I blinked. "I thought your middle name was Aloysius."

"We must hurry," Jonny said. "The Silver Swine plans to act tonight."

"What does the Swine plan to do?" I asked.

Beneath his helmet, I saw Jonny frown. "He has been collecting garbage and slops and disgusting waste matter for weeks. He plans to turn the entire town of Pupick Falls into a giant pigsty!"

"Oh no!" I gasped.

"Don't worry," Jonny said. "The glorious town of Pupick Falls will not become a pigsty—not on my watch!"

"Let's get going!" I cried. "By the way, how do we find the Silver Swine?"

"He's easy to find," Jonny replied. "He's a total pig."

JONNY PANTSFALLDOWN CONTINUED...

Since I'm the world's greatest sidekick (although I'm not perfect), I led the way. I lowered my head, sprang into the air, and flew out the front window.

"OWWWWWWWWWWWWWWWWW!"

Why can't I ever remember to open the window first?

When the agonizing pain faded and I stopped seeing double, I tugged the window open. Jonny and I then leapt—carefully—out into the night sky.

"YODEL-AY-EEE-OOOO!"

Johnny uttered his famous battle cry.

I gazed down at the ground below us. "Wow, I never get tired of flying," I said to Jonny Pantsfalldown. "Look at the people way down there. They look like ants!"

"They *are* ants," Jonny replied. "We need to fly a little higher."

We were nearly to town when a putrid odor hit us both. The stench was so strong, we dropped from the sky.

"Maybe I shouldn't have had beans for dinner!" I cried.

Jonny shook his head. "The Silver Swine has already begun his evil work," he said. "Look over there, Hairball. The Swine has flooded Main Street with pig slops and garbage. It's two feet deep!"

The smell was making my head spin.

"If we don't act fast," Jonny said, "the whole town of Pupick Falls will only be fit for hogs."

"We must find the Silver Swine," I said, struggling to breathe. "Is that him over there?" I pointed.

"Yes!" Jonny cried. "That's him—in person!"

Jonny had described the Silver Swine perfectly. He was a pig. An *actual pig*! And he must have weighed at least three hundred pounds. He wore a pink superhero cape and nothing else.

As Jonny and I strode toward him, the evil Swine started to grunt. A smile slowly crossed his snout.

"Are you proud of your work?" Johnny shouted at

him. "Well, don't be. Your work *stinks*! And I'm coming for you!"

"Please hurry," I said. "The smell is so bad, I can *taste* it!"

"YODEL-AY-EEE-OOOO!"

Jonny let out his world-famous battle cry—and took off running after the Silver Swine.

The huge pig swung around and started to run.

"You'll never get away!" Jonny called after it. "You're too big to run far!"

The Swine grunted and trotted away. But Jonny was closing in, running up close behind the evil villain.

And then . . . Jonny's Pants of Steel started to slip. The pants dropped to his thighs and then slid around his knees.

If only I had remembered the thumb tacks!

SPLOOOOOOSH.

Johnny fell face-first into the thick muck. He landed hard, sending up a wave of pig slop and waste and garbage. He disappeared under the surface for a while, then came up spluttering and choking, wiping the gunk off his face and helmet.

I watched in horror as the Silver Swine bounced around a corner and disappeared.

Jonny shook his fist in the air. "I'll get you next time, Swine!" he cried, spitting out mud. "No pig can do this to Pupick Falls. I'll get you—or my name isn't Jonny Pantsfalldown!"

That's our thrilling adventure for today, boys and girls. Until next time, this is the Mighty Hairball saying: "Keep your pants up—and reach for the stars!"

TWENTY-TWO

Adam Bomb here to tell you about our exciting next day at camp.

Morning sports activity was horseback riding, and we were totally pumped. "I always wanted to learn how to handle a horse," I said as we headed out of our cabin.

"I don't want to handle the horse," Cranky Frankie said. "I just want to ride it."

"Hey, guys—!" Nervous Rex called to us from the cabin. "Good luck. Remember, if you fall off your horse, try not to land on your head!"

"Good advice!" Cranky Frankie shouted back. "Is that what happened to you?"

That morning, Rex told us he could never get on a horse because he's allergic to big nostrils.

"I fell off a horse once and I did land on my head," Pat

Splat said. "Wow, was I embarrassed—I was on a merry-go-round!"

"I was on a merry-go-round once," Rob Slob said. "But I didn't enjoy it. I couldn't get the horse to stop going around in circles."

Up ahead, I saw that the girls had already arrived at the horse barn. Patty and Peter Perfect were standing off to one side. They were wearing riding outfits, funny-looking pants, little jackets, and boots that came all the way up their legs. And they each carried a riding crop that looked like a small whip.

They snapped their whips as we walked past, and then they burst out laughing. I guess they thought that was some kind of funny joke.

Luke Puke pinched his nose. "Ooh, gross. Why do you two smell so bad?" he asked the Perfects.

"We poured horse sweat all over our clothes so the horse would be friendly to us," Patty replied.

Luke squinted at them. "Horse sweat? Where did you get horse sweat?"

"We brought it from home," Peter answered.

"We like to be perfectly prepared," Patty added. "We saved some bottles just in case we ever rode a horse."

Brainy Janey was giving a talk about the history of horses. "The Palamoosa was the earliest known horse," Janey said. "A herd of Palamoosa were discovered running free on a beach in Montana. At least, that's what I read in the Wackipedia."

"When did they discover these horses?" Wacky Jackie asked her.

"It was in 1955," Janey said. "Before that, people only *dreamed* of horses."

Nasty Nancy rolled her eyes. "That can't be right," she said. "Who pulled the covered wagons across the west? Wasn't it horses?"

"That's only in the movies," Janey explained to her. "Who are you going to believe—me or the movies?"

"You should never argue with Brainy Janey," Wacky

Jackie said. "She's so smart, she learned how to sleep-read."

"Scientists still have one big question about horses," Janey continued. "When it comes to the Mustang—which came first? The car or the horse?"

We didn't have time to think about that. Head Counselor Mama was stomping out from around the horse barn, and her big biker boots were pounding the ground. She was swinging her cane in front of her as she strode toward us.

"Are you dumb cluck-clucks ready to mount up and ride?" she shouted.

"Yessss!" Pat Splat exclaimed enthusiastically.

Mama swung her cane and smacked him on the back of the head.

SPLAAAAAAT.

"Don't speak when I speak to you!" she cried. "That wasn't a question you were supposed to answer, you nit-nit!"

"S-sorry," Pat stammered, rubbing the back of his head.

"Now listen up, dodos!" Mama said, eyeing us one at a time. "I'm only going to say this once. And then I'm going to repeat it and repeat it."

"I don't get that," Wacky Jackie said.

Mama let out an angry cry and swung her cane at Wacky Jackie.

Jackie ducked, and the cane smacked Pat Splat in the gut.

"OWWWWW." Pat grabbed his belly and went down on his hands and knees.

"Show some respect!" Mama cried. "I only yell because I care!"

None of us dared say anything to that.

Mama spiked the cane into the ground between her biker boots and leaned on it. "Now listen up, freakanoids. I don't want to see any more violence. Understand?"

"But—" I started, but quickly stopped myself.

"If I see any more cane swinging," Mama continued, "I'll have to punish you all."

We all stared at her in terrified silence.

"If you get five demerits," Mama said, "you are no longer in the running to be Camp Champ."

More terrified silence.

Mama swept a hand through her purple hair. "I have an announcement to make," she said. "I know the camp promised horseback riding for everyone. But the horse died last summer."

We groaned in disappointment.

"But, no worries," Mama said. "Camp Lemme-Owttahere keeps its promises. We are all going air horseback riding this morning."

She raised her cane in the air and waited for one of us to say something. But we all just stared at her, and no one made a sound. Except for Rob Slob, who burped.

Mama shot him a dirty look. "Listen to me, chick-chicks," she said. "Air horseback riding can be a *blast*— if you follow the rules and learn how to ride correctly. It's a skill, just like falling off a bike."

Mama frowned and shook her head. "Speaking of that, last summer, two dum-diddies fell off their air horses.

And it wasn't pretty. So listen to Mama. Don't put the air horse before the air cart. Keep your air horses at a trot and don't ride recklessly."

Babbling Brooke raised her hand. "Do we each get our own air horse?" she asked.

Mama nodded. "The camp has generously decided to give each of you your own air horse."

Brooke clapped her hands. "Yaaay. I'm going to name mine Ginger!" she exclaimed.

"Why are you naming him Ginger?" I asked her.

"Because that's his name," she replied.

Mama pressed her fists against the sides of her head. "Everyone, please stop talking. The sound of kids' voices gives me a headache. I didn't want to be a counselor. I wanted a good job, like cleaning toilets. But that position was already taken."

She then wrapped her hands around invisible reins and patted the side of her invisible horse. "This is my air horse," she said. "His name is Biter. Can you guess why?"

No one answered.

"Now watch carefully, cluck-clucks," Mama said. "Follow my lead, and I'll have you riding in no time!"

TWENTY-THREE

Mama swung her leg over the saddle on her air horse. "Always mount on the left side," she instructed. "Just like this."

She stood erect. "Never try to mount from the rear. Your air horse will kick you from here to the lake."

Mama tugged on the invisible reins. "Okay, everyone, mount up!" she cried.

We all obediently climbed onto our air horses.

Nasty Nancy was muttering to herself. "My horse is limping," she said. "Why do I always get the lame air horse?"

"You're lucky," Cranky Frankie said. "Check out *my* air horse. I can't tell the front from the back!"

"Let's ride!" Mama cried. She slapped the side of her horse and took off, making galloping sounds with her lips. We followed her around the field and down to the beach.

In front of me, Junkfood John stopped suddenly. He jumped off his air horse and stood with his hand raised.

"John, what are you doing?" I asked. "I nearly rode right into you."

"I'm giving my horse some sugar cubes," John said. "Horses like sugar cubes."

Up ahead, I heard Cranky Frankie shout at Babbling Brooke. "Move it!" he cried. "Your horse is too slow!"

He gave her air horse a hard kick—and it galloped off with Brooke screaming and struggling to get control.

"I'll help you, Brooke!" Pat Splat called. He galloped after her, and his air horse ran smack into a tree.

SPLAAAAAT.

Wacky Jackie rode up beside me. Her eyes went wide and she pointed into the distance. "Hey, look, Adam! There's a *real* horse!"

I shielded my eyes with one hand and squinted. "No," I said. "That's not a horse. It's Rob Slob. And he *really* needs to take a bath! He's starting to become part of the forest."

"Hey, Mama—watch this!" Patty Perfect cried. She pulled up straight, then leaned back as far as she could and jumped up and down. "I taught my air horse some tricks!"

"Check this out!" Peter Perfect cried. "Patty and I trained our horses to do jumping tricks." He leaped over a small shrub.

Then he raised both hands high above his head and ran in a wide circle. "Mama, look—no hands!"

"Hold onto the reins, you dip-dip!" Mama shouted.

Peter laughed. "Patty and I are Camp Champs already!" he cried.

He and Patty slapped their legs to make horse-galloping sounds, and they rode off to their two-bedroom tent.

"How come they're so good at air horse riding?" Babbling Brooke asked.

"They probably took lessons back home," I said.

Mama climbed off her air horse and blew a loud whistle. "Horseback riding is over for today," she shouted.

We all came to a stop.

"Listen up, you dum-diddies," Mama said, waving her cane in the air. "I'll see you here tomorrow for our first air soccer game."

"We don't use a ball?" Pat Splat asked.

Mama swung her cane and slapped him hard behind the knees.

"No. No ball," she said. "We don't want anyone to get hurt."

TWENTY-FOUR

Nervous Rex here. I'm going to do my best to tell you what happened next.

It always makes me nervous to tell a story. I'm afraid I'll leave something out or get something wrong. It's a lot of p-pressure.

I was in our cabin under the bed, waiting for the guys to get back from horseback riding.

I kept thinking, maybe I should leave the cabin and go outside one of these days. But why take a chance?

The door swung open, and Adam Bomb stomped in, followed by the others. I could see that Adam was in an angry mood. He was red-faced and panting hard.

He kept puffing his red cheeks in and out. And he curled and uncurled his fists in front of him.

Believe me, it made me nervous to see Adam like

that. I know what happens when he gets totally steamed. And it's no fun to be around.

Cranky Frankie walked over to his bunk. "Hey," he snapped, "who put all these cracker crumbs in my bed?"

Junkfood John pointed up to the top bunk. "They must have fallen out of my bed," he said. "I was eating up there."

"But there are literally *hundreds* of crumbs!" Cranky Frankie protested.

"I know," John said. "I was eating real fast, and I kept missing my mouth."

"I don't care about that!" Adam Bomb screamed.

I wanted to duck back under my bed. Screaming makes me nervous, even when they're not screaming at *me*.

Adam shook his fists in the air. "I can't take it anymore!" he shouted. His face darkened until it was as purple as a plum.

"No worries. I'll get rid of the cracker crumbs," Junkfood John said.

"I'M NOT TALKING ABOUT THE CRUMBS!" Adam shrieked.

We all grew silent. I wanted to hide, but if I did, how could I tell you the story?

Adam punched the cabin wall. "I can't take one more minute of the Perfect twins!" he cried. "They win everything *at* school by being so . . . perfect. They win everything *out* of school. And now—"

Adam started to choke. Rob Slob slapped him on the back until he started breathing again.

"And now," Adam continued, "we're at summer camp—*and they are winning everything here, too!*"

His eyes bulged. His face grew even redder. "I . . . I can't STAND it!" he shrieked.

And then he exploded.

All over the cabin.

TWENTY-FIVE

I jumped onto the nearest bunk and pulled the pillow over my head.

Watching your friend explode can be very upsetting. I hadn't felt this nervous since I poured the milk into my breakfast cereal this morning.

When I finally looked out, Pat Splat and Luke Puke were carrying the pieces of Adam Bomb to a bunk in the corner. They tried to arrange him so he looked like himself. But it wasn't easy.

"Adam is right," Luke Puke said. "We have to find a way to beat the Perfects. We can't let them become Camp Champs this summer."

Junkfood John squinted at him. "Excuse me? What did you say?" John asked. "These tortilla chips I'm eating are crunching so loud, I can't hear a word you are saying."

Cranky Frankie groaned. "John, did you ever think of chewing with your mouth closed?"

"Is that *allowed*?" he asked.

I heard a knock on the cabin door. Handy Sandy poked her head in.

"John, what on earth are you eating?" she demanded.

"We can hear you chewing across the lake in the girls' cabin."

"I like a good crunch," John said to her.

Sandy stepped into the cabin. "Where's Adam?"

I pointed to the bunk against the wall. "M-most of him is over there, in that bed," I said.

"Adam exploded," Luke Puke explained.

Sandy slapped her forehead. "Again?"

We all nodded.

"Are you sure you collected all of him this time?" Sandy asked. She pointed. "What's that leg under the bed?"

"It's just a leg," Rob Slob explained. "It was there when we got here. Really."

"What made Adam so upset?" Sandy asked.

"The Perfects. What else?" Cranky Frankie said, rolling his eyes.

"We have to find a way to stop them," Luke Puke said. "We have to stop them from being Camp Champs this summer."

A smile crossed Handy Sandy's face. "Don't worry," she said. "I have an idea."

TWENTY-SIX

Babbling Brooke here. If I may, allow me to continue our story.

Chef Indy Jestian served dinner in the mess hall. We ate some kind of roasted animal chops and potato-less potato salad, which was gooey but awesome.

I wanted to do my food cheer again . . .

GIVE ME AN F!

GIVE ME A U!

GIVE ME A D!

GIVE ME AN E . . .

But I was too busy trying to chew the chops to stand up and lead a cheer. The chops were really tough. Junkfood John pounded his chop on the table, and it made a dent in the wood.

Rob Slob leaned across the table toward me. He

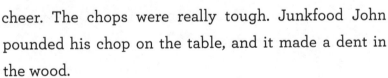

had a playful grin on his face. "Brooke, know what kids always like to do at camp?" he whispered.

I shook my head. "No. What?"

"Food fights," he whispered. "They are a riot. All campers like food fights."

I stared at him. "Are you serious?"

"Watch this," Rob said, and raised his dinner plate in the air. "Food fight!" he shouted. "Food fight, everyone!"

Rob heaved his plate of chops at kids at the other end of the long table.

The plate bounced off the table, hit the wall, and shattered. And the chops and potato-less salad flew all over the floor.

Everyone turned to Rob.

There was silence.

No one joined in.

Everyone just stared.

Rob Slob shrugged. "Guess food fights aren't as popular as I thought," he said.

He then turned to the end of the table. "Can anyone throw my food back to me? I'm still hungry."

For dessert, we had something the chef called Bird Pie.

I wish he had told us what was in it.

After dinner, we all gathered in front of the small stage at the back of the mess hall. The Perfect twins wanted to perform some kind of show for us.

I sat next to Nasty Nancy. "What are the twins going to do?" I whispered.

"I don't know," Nancy replied. "But I'm sure it will be perfect." She snickered. "Perfectly *awful.*"

I guess that was some kind of joke, but I didn't really get it.

Behind me, Leaky Lindsay sneezed really hard, and I felt the back of my T-shirt get wet. I turned around and she sneezed again. So now the *front* of my T-shirt was wet, too.

Lindsay was using a floor mat as a tissue, but it didn't seem to help.

Just then, the Perfect twins stepped onto the stage. Peter carried a thick rope in his hands.

"Tonight, we're going to demonstrate some perfect knot-tying," Patty said.

"Tying knots can be very entertaining," Peter said. "And it can be useful, too. You never know when you'll need a knot."

"We think tying knots is educational," Patty Perfect said. "Watch carefully, and you may be able to tie knots almost as good as we do."

"Of course, you won't be perfect like Patty and I," Peter added. "But you can do your best."

Peter raised a rope in both hands. "First, you must always start out with a rope," Patty said. "We find that a rope is best for tying knots."

"The first knot we're going to show you is called a Granny Knot," Peter said. "That's because the rope is as wrinkled as your granny!"

Was that supposed to be a joke? I couldn't tell. I'm not good with jokes—especially when I don't know if it's a joke or not.

Peter Perfect tugged the ends of the rope into a bow, then reversed the bow, and then turned the whole thing upside down in his hands. Then he held it up for all of us to see. "A perfect Granny Knot!" he exclaimed. "I couldn't do it any better!"

"Peter, you couldn't do it any better," his sister said, "because it's *perfect*!"

"Why thank you, Patty. And so are you."

Patty then took the rope from her brother. "Now I will show you all how to tie a Sailor's Knot," she announced. "It's called a Sailor's Knot because if you don't tie it right, you get seasick!"

Was that another joke?

Patty twisted the rope and curled it in on itself and twisted it some more. Then she held it up. "Here it is—a perfect Sailor's Knot."

We all stared at them. It looked a lot like the Granny Knot to me.

Next, the twins did a Rip Knot, a Doggy Knot, a Cheese-and-Crackers Knot, and a Knot Knot.

"Thank you! Thank you!" Patty cried. She then took a bow, even though no one was clapping. "You're a great audience."

Everyone started to yawn loudly.

"You don't have to beg us," Peter said. "We'll do one more knot for you. It's our famous Slippery Knot."

Kids groaned and then yawned some more.

"We want to demonstrate our Slippery Knot on Uncle Cousin," Patty said. "Let's see if he can slip out of it."

Peter shielded his eyes with one hand. "Uncle Cousin, where are you? Come on up here."

We all looked around. But there was no sign of Uncle Cousin.

"We'll go get him," Patty Perfect said, and she and her brother stepped down from the stage.

That's when Handy Sandy moved beside me. "Brooke, listen," she whispered. "Here's my plan . . ."

TWENTY-SEVEN

Handy Sandy leaned in close and whispered. "Brooke, are you enjoying the knot-tying demonstration?"

I shook my head. "I like balloon animals better," I said. "Balloon animals are my favorite. I mean, how do you make a dachshund out of only three balloons?"

"Well, the Perfects think they're scoring points by showing off all these knots," Sandy whispered. "Maybe we can make sure they're *not* so perfect."

I squinted at her. "What do you plan to do?"

Sandy gazed around. Kids were standing up and stretching, talking and laughing, and moving around the mess hall. "No one is watching," she whispered.

Sandy jumped up, crept to the stage, and took the rope the Perfects had left on the stage floor. Then she hurried back to me.

"Sandy, what are you doing with their rope?" I asked.

She raised a finger to her lips. "Sssshhh. I brought a tube of Wacky Glue."

"Wacky Glue?"

Sandy nodded and pulled the little tube of glue from the pocket of her shorts. "I'm just going to put a little dab of glue on the rope," she whispered. "So their Slippery Knot won't slip. This will be awesome."

"Are you sure it will work?" I asked.

"It can't fail," Sandy said. "It will *totally* embarrass them! What could go wrong?"

She held the rope in one hand. Then she tilted the tube of Wacky Glue over it and squeezed out a big glob.

"Hurry. They're coming back!" I whispered.

Sandy quickly shoved the glue back into her pocket.

"We found Uncle Cousin!" Patty Perfect exclaimed. She and her brother were guiding the camp owner to the stage. "Take your seats, everyone. The Slippery Knot is our best knot."

Everyone sat back down in front of the stage except for Handy Sandy. "Another volunteer," Patty Perfect said and stuck out her hand. "Hand me the rope, please."

Sandy stuck her hand out toward Patty.

Patty frowned at her. "The rope, *please.*"

Sandy was about to give the rope to Patty. Then she shook her hand up and down, but the rope remained.

"Sandy, we all want to see this knot," Uncle Cousin said. "Hand the rope to Patty."

Sandy shook her hand up and down some more. She grabbed the rope with her other hand and tugged. "Sorry," she said finally. "It's stuck."

"Huh?" Patty Perfect stared in disbelief. "Stuck?"

"I think I used too much Wacky Glue," Sandy muttered.

"Let me try," Uncle Cousin said. He grabbed the rope in both hands and pulled as hard as he could.

He pulled so hard, Sandy nearly fell over. But the rope stayed stuck to her hand.

"It sure is stuck tight," Uncle Cousin said. He turned to the audience. "Anyone have any ideas on how to get the rope off her hand?"

Mama stood up. "How about a hacksaw?" she said.

Uncle Cousin shook his head. "That might get messy," he replied. He then turned back to Sandy. "Tell you what. Let's just wait for the glue to soften."

Sandy squinted at him. "Soften? How long will that take?"

"It should loosen up in a year or two," Uncle Cousin told her.

TWENTY-EIGHT

Leaky Lindsay here. I'm new to all of this, but for some reason they've asked me to continue the story.

Later that night, **AHCHOO**.

I mean **AHHHHCHHHOOOOO**.

We all got together and **AHHHCHOOOOOEY**. **AHCHOOO**.

Anyone have a tissue?

ACHOO ACHOO.

I'm sorry. I can't do this. I—

TWENTY-NINE

Wacky Jackie here. Well that was . . . unpleasant. But now I get to continue the story.

We gave Leaky Lindsay a bedsheet to use as a tissue. Then, later that night, we all crept out of our cabins and met on the steps to the mess hall.

It was a warm, clear night. A big half-moon sent down silvery light from high in the sky. Crickets chirped all around. At least, I think they were crickets.

What else chirps like that?

It was exciting to be out so late. We knew it was against the rules, but we were desperate—we had to think of a way to stop the Perfect twins.

The mess hall was closed and dark, and we all huddled together in front of the door. Everyone except for Nervous Rex. He wouldn't leave the cabin at night. He said darkness makes him itch.

Handy Sandy kept tugging at the rope stuck to her hand. "I think it will come off in warm water," she said. "Or maybe cold water. I'm not sure which."

Rob Slob sat next to me. I'm used to his smell, so it was no big deal. He wasn't wearing a shirt, and I noticed a bunch of long, black spots on his chest.

"No worries," Rob said. "It's just some dirt."

Brainy Janey leaned close to Rob and inspected his chest. "No, that's not dirt," she said. "Those are leeches. You probably got them in the lake."

Rob lowered his eyes to look. "Leeches?"

"You probably should pull them off," Janey told him. "Leeches suck your blood."

"So *that's* why I felt a little itchy today," Rob said.

He flicked a fat, juicy one off his chest and it went flying into the air.

SPLAAAAAT.

It landed on Pat Splat's head.

"Let's get down to business," Nasty Nancy said. "I need my beauty sleep."

Cranky Frankie tossed his head back and burst out laughing.

"What are *you* laughing about?" Nancy demanded.

"I'm laughing about something you said," Frankie

replied, and giggled some more. "You're funny. *Beauty sleep.*"

"I have a good idea for stopping Peter and Patty Perfect," Brainy Janey interrupted.

We all leaned closer to listen.

"It involves covering them in large reptiles," she said.

"Janey, where will we get reptiles?" I asked.

She crossed her arms in front of her. "I can't think of *everything*!" she snapped.

"Maybe the Smellville Zoo will lend us some reptiles," Babbling Brooke said.

"There's only one problem," Cranky Frankie

said. "The Smellville Zoo doesn't have any animals, remember? They sold them all to raise awareness for animal conservation."

"That's why it's no fun to go to the zoo anymore," I said. "I knew there was a good reason."

"Are those really *leeches* on Rob Slob?" Luke Puke asked.

He's always a little behind the rest of us.

"Yes, those are leeches," Janey told him. "But they're harmless . . . as long as they are on someone else."

Rob made an **ULLLLP** sound, pressed his hand over his mouth, and ran around to the side of the building to puke his guts out.

"We can't let the Perfects win Camp Champ again," Nasty Nancy said. "It will ruin our summer."

She pointed across the campgrounds to the big, white two-room tent with a hot tub, where the Perfects lived. "I'll bet they're sound asleep in there," Nancy said, "dreaming about how they already won Camp Champ."

"We could sneak into their tent and give them my leeches," Rob Slob said. "Then they wouldn't be perfect anymore."

"I don't think that would stop them," Brainy Janey said. "Not as much as their being smothered in reptiles."

Handy Sandy tried to snap her fingers, but the rope was in the way. "I think I have an idea," she said, raising her rope hand. "I still have plenty of Wacky Glue left. What if we sneak over and glue their tent flaps shut?"

"What would that do?" I asked.

"The Perfects will be trapped inside," Sandy said. "They won't be able to get out of their tent. And they will miss the air soccer game tomorrow morning."

"Brilliant!" Babbling Brooke gushed. "We'll win the game, and they'll be losers. You're a genius!" She jumped up, tossed her hands above her head, and did a silent cheer.

"Let's do it," Brainy Janey said. "That idea is almost as good as reptiles."

So . . . that's what we did.

Handy Sandy hurried back to the girls' cabin and got her tube of Wacky Glue. Then we all sneaked over to the Perfects' tent.

"*Sssshhh.*" We kept reminding one another to be silent. "*Sshhh.*"

"*Sssssshh.*"

"*Sssshhhhh.*"

It's a wonder all the *sshhhhhs* didn't wake up Peter and Patty.

Handy Sandy carefully squeezed a thick layer of glue onto the tent flaps. Then Rob Slob and Cranky Frankie pressed the flaps together until they stuck tight.

"The Perfects will never get out," Rob said. "No way they are strong enough to push their way through. Someone will have to rescue them. And then they'll be totally embarrassed."

"Let's make sure the tent doesn't have other openings," Brainy Janey said.

Walking on tiptoe, we silently moved all around the tent.

"Ssssshhhh."

"Ssssshhhhh."

No back opening. No side openings.

"They are trapped in there," Babbling Brooke said. "We win!" She leaped into the air and did another silent cheer.

We went back to our cabins, giggling, and congratulated ourselves for being geniuses.

"We win! We win!" Babbling Brooke continued to cheer as we got changed for bed.

THIRTY

The next morning, we girls hurried to the mess hall for breakfast. But Peter and Patty Perfect were already at a table. They waved to us as we stared back at them in shock.

Who could believe it?

Handy Sandy strode over to their table. She pressed her hands against her sides and stared at them. "How did you get out of your tent?" she demanded.

Peter swallowed a forkful of scrambled egg substitute. "We used the basement door," he said.

Sandy slapped her own forehead. "Basement door? Your tent has a *basement*?"

"Of course," Patty Perfect replied. "Where else would we put our air conditioner?"

"These blackberries are terrific," Peter said, raising

his spoon. "Patty and I always eat eighteen berries a day for good nutrition."

"Once I slipped up," Patty said, "and only ate seventeen blackberries. I was hungry for the rest of the day."

"Have a good breakfast," Peter said, then turned to his sister. "How many blackberries have I eaten? They made me lose count."

We slumped to our table, sighing in defeat. From across the room, we watched Peter and Patty having their perfect breakfast.

"We'll think of another plan," Brainy Janey said. "There are a thousand things we can do to stop them from being Camp Champ."

"Name one," Nasty Nancy said.

"Give me time to wake up my brilliant brain," Janey said. "This morning is free swim in Lake Bleccch. I'm sure we can think up at least a dozen ways to embarrass them in the water."

"Name one," Nasty Nancy said again.

Janey started to answer. But the mess hall door swung open, and the boys came marching in—with Adam Bomb leading the way.

"Adam! You're back!" I cried.

Adam took a short bow. "I pulled myself together," he said. "So, what did I miss?"

"Not much," Nasty Nancy told him. "The Perfects are still perfect."

"There must be a way to stop them from being Camp Champ," Adam said.

"Name one," Nasty Nancy replied.

Brainy Janey shot her a look. "You're so not helpful," she added.

The boys sat down at the table next to ours. Junkfood John held up a big brown jar. "I brought extra maple syrup," he said.

"We're having eggs," I told him. "We're not having pancakes."

"That's okay," John said. "I just like drinking syrup." He opened the jar, tilted it over his mouth, and drank it all down.

Then he began swatting the air with both hands. "Why are all these flies swarming me?" John cried.

"Maybe because you spilled syrup all over your face?" I said.

"No," John replied, "that's not the reason. I think it's because I'm sitting next to Rob Slob."

He was right. The flies must have been drawn by the smell of garbage. Rob's normal smell.

"Where is Nervous Rex?" Babbling Brooke asked. "Is he coming out of the cabin today?"

Adam Bomb shook his head. "Rex won't come out. He doesn't want to swim in Lake Bleccch. He said water gives him the heebie-jeebies."

"What are heebie-jeebies?" I asked.

"I don't know," Rob Slob answered. "But I think I have a couple of them climbing up my neck."

Brainy Janey snapped her fingers. "Oh wow," she said. "Wow oh wow. Rob, you just gave me an awesome, brilliant, award-winning, amazing, astounding, gob-smacking idea. And did I mention brilliant?"

I leaned across the table. "Janey, what's your idea?" I asked.

THIRTY-ONE

Leaky Lindsay here. I'm going to do my best to continue the story.

Janey gazed around the table. She—

AHCHOOOOOO.

AHCHOOOOOEY. AHCHOOOOEY.

AHHHHCHOOO.

Sorry, I can't do this.

Please don't choose me again.

THIRTY-TWO

Cranky Frankie here. Great. Now it's up to *me* to continue the story. Well, here goes nothing.

We gave Leaky Lindsay a tablecloth to use as a tissue. "Are you *sure* you no longer have a cold?" I asked her.

Lindsay had sneezed all over her breakfast. And mine. "I think so," she said.

We turned back to Brainy Janey to continue telling us her big plan.

"Remember yesterday?" Janey said.

"What day was that?" Wacky Jackie asked.

"It was yesterday," Janey replied.

"Are you sure?" Jackie asked.

"Am I sure of *what*?" Janey demanded.

"Sure it was yesterday?" Jackie said.

I squinted at Jackie. "Can I make a polite request?" I asked her.

"Of course. What's your polite request?" Jackie said.

"Shut yer yap."

"That wasn't polite," Wacky Jackie said. "Not even a little."

"Oh. Sorry," I replied. "Shut yer yap, *please*."

"That's better."

Brainy Janey started again. "Yesterday, Head Counselor Mama told us about Lake Bleccch," she began. "She said we were going to have free swim this morning. And she warned us about the Lake Bleccch Monster. Remember?"

"What day was that?" Wacky Jackie asked.

I dumped my eggs over her head, but she didn't seem to notice.

"It was yesterday," Janey replied. "Mama said it was a camp legend. The Lake Bleccch Monster has been spotted by campers many times over the years."

Peter and Patty Perfect finished their breakfast. They waved to us with perfect smiles on their faces, and their teeth gleamed brightly in the morning light. Janey stopped talking until they were out the door.

"The Lake Bleccch Monster is a big, hairy creature that lives underwater on the bottom of the lake," Janey said. "Mama said sometimes it rises to the

surface, roaring and snarling, searching for something to eat."

"Are you sure she wasn't talking about Junkfood John," I asked.

Janey ignored me. "Do you remember the warning from Head Counselor Mama?" she asked. "Mama said if you see the monster, that means it's hungry. And to swim for your life."

"Mama should shut her yap," I said. "She was just trying to scare us."

"No way," Babbling Brooke said. "Mama is too kind. Why would she want to scare us?"

"What planet are you living on?" I asked her.

"It doesn't matter," Brainy Janey said. "This is how we are going to ruin Peter and Patty's swim."

We all grew silent, eagerly waiting to hear Janey's idea.

She turned to Rob Slob, who was busy batting away flies.

"Listen, Rob," Janey said. "When we get into the lake, you wait till no one is looking. Then you dive under the water."

"Then what?" Rob said. "I stay there?"

"No," Janey replied. "You burst up with a deafening

roar right behind Patty and Peter. They will think *you* are the Lake Bleccch Monster, and they will *scream like babies!*"

"Brilliant!" Babbling Brooke cried. "Brilliant!"

"They'll scream like babies, and everyone will laugh at them. And their chances will be ruined," Janey said.

"Brilliant!" Brooke gushed again. "You're brilliant!"

"I'll do it," Rob Slob said. "I always wanted to be a monster. It's on my bucket list."

"What day is this?" Wacky Jackie asked.

THIRTY-THREE

Adam Bomb here—back and better than ever (except for the dizziness).

We were all excited about our plan to scare the Perfect twins and ruin their chances of being Camp Champs. Brainy Janey had done it again.

Babbling Brooke wanted to do a cheer. So she jumped up and started to make one up:

"GIVE ME A B!

"WHAT RHYMES WITH B?

"ANYONE HAVE ANY SUGGESTIONS?"

It wasn't a very good cheer. And we didn't have time to finish it. We had to change into our swimsuits and get to the lake.

Back in the cabin, I asked Nervous Rex if he wanted to come out and swim. He started to shake and said,

"Water makes me nervous. Once, I almost drowned sipping from a water fountain."

Rex hadn't seen the sun for days. Moss was starting to grow on his back. At least, I think it was moss. He might have been wearing one of Rob Slob's shirts.

The rest of us changed and hurried to Lake Bleccch.

Head Counselor Mama was waiting for us on the shore. And we could see the girls trotting over from their cabin on the other side of the lake.

Patty and Peter Perfect wore matching red swimsuits and were slapping sunscreen on each other. "Working on our perfect tan," Peter said.

"We always do stretching exercises before we get in the water," Patty said. "Muscle tone is very important if you want to be as perfect as we are."

Cranky Frankie picked up a clump of soft dirt, made a mudball, and heaved it at them. But he missed, and it smacked Pat Splat on the back of the head instead.

SPLAAAAAT.

"Do you cluck-clucks know how to swim?" Mama asked.

We all raised our hands.

"I don't really care," Mama said. "But if one of you drowns, I might get in trouble."

"Is the water cold?" Wacky Jackie asked.

"Does a camel have lips?" Mama answered.

That didn't make any sense, but I didn't want to be the one to tell her. She had her cane stretched out in one hand. And I knew she liked to use it to make a point.

Mama had a silver whistle hanging from her neck. She picked it up with her other hand. "When I blow the whistle, everyone *in* the water," she said. "And when I blow it again, everyone *out* of the water. Is that clear?"

Wacky Jackie raised her hand. "Is that in or out?"

"Is *what* in or out?" Mama snapped.

Jackie shrugged. "Just asking."

"First whistle blow—in the water," Mama said. "Second blow—out of the water."

"What if we are *already* out of the water?" Jackie said. "What do we do when we hear the second whistle blow? Get *back* in the water?"

Mama frowned and shook her head. "No. Don't go back in."

"What if we didn't hear the first whistle blow and we didn't get in the water?" Jackie asked.

"You'll hear it," Mama said. She brought her face close to Wacky Jackie and blew the whistle right in Jackie's ear.

"Whoa!" Jackie jumped a mile in the air and came down shaking her head. "What did *that* whistle

blow mean?" she asked Mama. "Should I get in the water?"

Mama **GRRRRRED** like an angry tiger. "Okay, you bim-bums. Just follow my instructions."

"What were your instructions?" Junkfood John asked. "I was chewing these Oyster Crunch Bites so loud I couldn't hear."

Head Counselor Mama let out an exasperated groan. Then she turned to Handy Sandy and pointed to something that Sandy was holding. "What have you got there?" she demanded.

Sandy held it up in front of her. "I made my own goggles," she said.

Sandy is so handy, she can make anything. One morning, she made waffles out of pancakes. Now *that's* clever!

Mama squinted at the goggles. "What are they made out of?" she asked.

Sandy raised them higher. "I used the bottoms of soda bottles," she said.

"But you can't see through them!" Mama declared.

"I still have a few kinks to work out," Sandy told her.

"Are we allowed to splash one another?" Nasty Nancy asked.

"That's against camp rules, nuk-nuk," Mama said. "Didn't you read page one hundred forty-three of the rule book? Campers are only allowed to splash themselves."

Patty Perfect held up a big red-and-white beach ball. "We brought our own beach ball from home," she said. "Peter and I never go in the water without a beach ball for perfect fun in the sun."

Cranky Frankie threw another mudball at the twins. But it slipped out of his hand and landed on his own head.

"Okay, lum-lums," Mama said. "Have a great swim. And don't pay any attention to the big clumps of green goo in the water. That's just a little bit of radioactive waste matter. It's really no big deal."

Mama raised the whistle to her mouth and blew. Then we all stampeded toward the water. But we stopped and turned back when the whistle kept whistling.

Mama was struggling to pull the whistle from her mouth, but it wouldn't stop.

The shrill sound rose like a siren and whistled and whistled and whistled.

Mama dropped her cane and used both hands to tug at the whistle string.

I cried out when she swallowed the *string*, too!

GULLLLP.

We could see it slide down her throat!

Mama gasped and made choking sounds.

And the whistle kept whistling. It was in her stomach and *still* whistling.

Mama tried to control her breathing, but the whistle just kept on going.

We all gathered around and stared at her, wondering what we should do.

Wacky Jackie raised her hand. "Mama," she said, "how will we know when to get out of the water?"

Mama got so angry at Jackie, she started to hiccup. And the next thing we knew, the whistle *and the string* came out. And then she reached for her cane.

THIRTY-FOUR

I ran into the water. I was already up to my knees when I realized it was freezing cold. Gobs of radioactive waste were coating my legs, but it was too late to turn back.

Brainy Janey dove under the surface. When she came up, she flashed me the thumbs-up signal. We both knew what was about to happen. The Perfect twins would have their swim ruined. And we were all going to have a good laugh before being declared Camp Champs.

The morning sun was high in the sky. And I got used to the cold water very quickly. I swam out from the shore, and then floated on my back for a while.

It felt awesome. I think everyone was happy and excited for our first swim.

Peter and Patty Perfect swam in a circle around us, demonstrating different strokes. "This is a sidestroke," Peter said, swimming on his side. He turned over. "And this is the *other* sidestroke. I do it perfectly because I'm a natural water person."

You'll be stroking for your life in a minute, I thought. I couldn't wait for the big moment. *Rob Slob, do your thing!*

"We don't do the butterfly stroke," Patty said. "We do the *monarch* butterfly stroke. It's a lot prettier."

She splashed around for a while, showing us the monarch butterfly stroke. Then she and her brother tossed their beach ball back and forth, sending it higher and higher and batting it to each other perfectly.

Come on, come on, I thought. *It's scare time!*

We were all watching the twins. We knew what was about to happen, and we were ready.

And then . . . it happened.

A booming roar rose up from the water. The whole lake seemed to shake as a huge surge formed, growing taller—until a high wave burst behind the Perfect twins.

They screamed—we *all* screamed—as an enormous, hairy beast burst up from beneath the surface. It raised its ugly head in a furious roar and slapped the water so hard, another high wave shot up into the sky.

I tried to hide my laughter. "Awesome!" I told myself. "It's working!"

Patty and Peter Perfect were frantically swimming for their lives. I don't know what stroke they were doing, but they were crying and shrieking and screaming in fright the whole way.

The rest of us were laughing out loud now. We were slapping high-fives in the water and grinning at one another, our thumbs up all the way.

"Rob Slob was *awesome*!" Brainy Janey shouted. "Good work, Rob!"

We were all feeling terrific. What a triumph!

But then I turned—and saw Rob Slob standing on the shore.

"I had to go back to the cabin and get my goggles," he shouted. "Is it too late to scare the Perfect twins?"

Well, I'm not exactly sure about *what* happened in the lake. Maybe that was a camper from last year who spent too much time in the radioactive waste. Or . . . maybe there really *is* a Lake Bleccch monster.

But we were all seriously freaked.

There was only one thing to do to calm down. Go back to the cabin—and watch another episode of *Jonny Pantsfalldown*.

JONNY PANTSFALLDOWN

Favorite TV superhero of Wacky Jackie and Junkfood John

Episode 2,045

Hold on to your pants, everyone! And keep your belt buckled tight for ADVENTURE! It's time for another action-packed episode of JONNY PANTSFALLDOWN.

That's me standing beside him—the World's Greatest Sidekick—THE MIGHTY HAIRBALL!

It's night in the town of Pupick Falls. A time of quiet. A time of darkness. A time when the criminals come out to play. But *crime doesn't play*—not when Jonny Pantsfalldown is on duty.

With his Pants of Steel, Jonny protects the town whenever he isn't busy with something else. When people hear his mighty battle cry . . .

"YODEL-AY-EEE-OOO!"

. . . it means law and order will probably be returned as best as Jonny can.

As Jonny always says, "You can't spell *superhero* without *up*." And by that, he means without keeping his *pants* up.

And that's why *I'm* here. I graduated in the top third of my class in Sidekick School. And yes, I wear my underpants on the outside of my costume. But so does every other sidekick!

Tonight, I found Jonny in his dressing room, preparing for crime-fighting duty. "Jonny," I said, "what terrifying villain will we be going after tonight?"

"**ARRRRRRRGGGGH,**" he replied.

"I never heard of that one," I said. "Is he new in town?"

"**ARRRRGGGGGHHHH,**" Jonny said. "**AAAARGGGGH. AAAARGGGGH.**"

It was then that I realized his toothbrush was stuck in his throat. Like all superheroes, Jonny is devoted to clean teeth. But sometimes he goes too far.

I yanked the toothbrush from his throat—the way I was trained in Sidekick School. Jonny choked and

gagged for about ten minutes. Then he turned to me and spoke in his booming voice. A voice so powerful that it turns apples into cider.

"I forgot to rinse," he said.

When he returned from the sink, he was almost ready for action. I took a hand towel and dried off his chin for him.

"Hairball," he said, "tonight we go after one of the meanest villains we have ever pursued."

"How mean is he?" I asked.

"He's so mean," Jonny replied, "I've seen him step on a ladybug. Deliberately."

"No!" I gasped.

Then I accidentally burped up some of my dinner. Frog intestines don't always agree with me.

"Need a lozenge?" Jonny asked.

"No, I'm fine," I said. He's always so thoughtful and caring. "Jonny, tell me—who is this evil criminal? What is his name?"

"His name is . . . Billy Pantsfalldown," Jonny said.

"Oh no!" I gasped again. "Not your *brother*!"

"Actually, he's a second cousin," Jonny said. "But he's as evil as I am delightful."

"What does your evil Pantsfalldown cousin plan to do?" I asked.

"Billy is so mean," Jonny answered, "he plans to write a letter to the mayor—and misspell the mayor's name!"

"Huh?" I gasped again. It was a big night for gasping. My throat was starting to get dry. I popped in a throat lozenge after all. I sucked on it for a while before I realized it was actually one of my coat buttons.

"Billy Pantsfalldown is going to misspell the mayor's name—*deliberately*?" I finally choked out. "That's horrible!"

"We have to hurry," Jonny said. "He must be stopped."

"We can't allow his letter to reach Mayor Firtbaghovermeisterlizbergerling," I said. "He will be terribly upset if his name is misspelled. What do you plan to do, Jonny?"

"Take away Billy's pen," the great and mighty superhero boomed. His voice was so deep and powerful, my teeth loosened.

"We've got to hurry," Jonny said. "Don't bother with the door. Let's fly out the window."

"Good idea," I said, and took off.

I leaped into the air and heard a deafening crash as the window glass shattered. Startled, I fell to the floor. "I'm okay!" I cried.

I glanced in the mirror. I had a few cuts, but this was no time for injuries.

"It's the sidekick's job to *open* the window before we fly through it," Jonny scolded.

"My bad," I said.

JONNY PANTSFALLDOWN, CONTINUED...

We flew through the night sky. The moon was full, and the light hurt my eyes. I held my breath as we flew over the town. I always forget how airsick I get.

I was glad when Jonny signaled for us to land on the front lawn of a small house. A light was on in the front window. "That's him inside," Jonny said. "See? He just got up from his desk."

"Thank goodness we're in time," I said.

"YODEL-AY-EEE-OOO!"

Jonny shouted out his famous battle cry.

A few seconds later, Billy Pantsfalldown stepped

out of his house. In the silvery moonlight, I could see he was holding an envelope in one hand.

"Stop right there, Billy!" Jonny shouted. "Don't move!"

"You're too late, Cousin Jonny," Billy said. "The letter is already written, and I'm going to mail it now. And I misspelled Mayor Firtbaghovermeisterlizbergerling's name, just as I promised."

"You evil fiend! How did you spell it?" Jonny demanded.

"I spelled it with a Q!" Billy exclaimed, and he tossed back his head and laughed an evil laugh.

"You'll never get away with it!" Jonny shouted.

"Yes, I will! I'm on my way to the mailbox on the corner," Billy said. "And there's nothing you can do to stop me!" He then took off running across the front lawn.

Jonny leaned into the wind and bolted after his evil cousin. No one is faster than Jonny Pantsfalldown. The race wasn't even close. Jonny was catching up to Billy—when he suddenly turned back to me.

"Hey, Hairball—" he called. "We forgot the Velcro belt to hold up my Pants of Steel!"

"My bad," I said again.

Just then Jonny's pants slipped down and fell to his ankles. Jonny tripped over his pants and fell face-forward into a pile of mud.

"Hahahahaha!" Billy's laugh rang to the sky as he ran full speed toward the corner mailbox. And then *his* pants fell down, and he fell into the gutter beside the curb.

Jonny raised his face from the mud. And we both watched as the wind caught Billy's envelope and carried it higher and higher . . . into the woods.

"Another victory for the good guys!" Jonny cried, waving his muddy fists in the air. "Hairball, did you by any chance bring a towel?"

That's our thrilling adventure for today, boys and girls. Until next time, this is the Mighty Hairball saying: "Keep your pants up—and reach for the stars!"

THIRTY-FIVE

Brainy Janey here. And it's my turn again to continue telling you about our adventure at summer camp.

"Food fight!" Rob Slob shouted. And he heaved his plate of beans at the kids at the next table. "Food fight, everybody! Come on! Anybody? *Anybody?*"

The kids ignored Rob and kept eating and talking to one another.

No one else joined in, so Rob slammed his fists on the table. "What kind of camp is this? No one wants to throw food?"

Everyone continued to ignore him.

"Hey, can someone gather up those beans and send them back to me?" Rob asked. "I'm still hungry."

"I'll tell you something interesting, Rob," I said. "Beans aren't really beans. They're legumes."

Rob muttered a rude word that I won't repeat.

We were all eager to finish lunch because a big meeting was scheduled. Head Counselor Mama was about to tell us the plans for the big Lemme Talent Show. And after the talent show, the winner of the Camp Champ Award will be announced.

It was our last chance to stop the Perfect twins from winning this year. But how?

They were already practicing—riding on unicycles and juggling fire batons at the back of the mess hall.

The rest of us finished our lunch—cream of buffalo soup, stewed beans, and breaded fish parts—and gathered in front of the stage for the meeting.

"That was the best lunch we ever had," Rob Slob said. "Too bad I tossed my beans across the room."

Luke Puke made a disgusted face. "I barf up better food than that," he said.

"And what was up with the mashed seaweed we had last night?" Cranky Frankie said. "I thought it was overcooked."

"Your *brain* is overcooked!" Nasty Nancy said. It didn't make any sense, but it was nasty.

Junkfood John held up a large bag. "Would anyone like a Chocolate-Covered Meat Chip? They're chewy but good."

No one wanted one. So John stuffed his mouth, chewing hard.

Finally, Uncle Cousin stepped on the stage. He took a little bow even though no one clapped.

"Booyah, everyone!" he shouted. "Booyah!"

"Booyah!" a few of the other kids shouted back.

"Ricky ticky! Booyah!" he cried. "I love to see your enthusiasm! That's the camp spirit! Booyah!"

We all stared back at Uncle Cousin in silence.

"Get on with it!" Head Counselor Mama snapped from the side of the room. She banged her cane on the floor.

Uncle Cousin cleared his throat. He took a deep breath, and his face slowly turned red. "I'm afraid I have some bad news, campers," he said, shaking his head.

He took another breath. I thought I saw a teardrop slide down his round cheeks.

"I'm sorry to say we must close Camp Lemme-Owttahere after tomorrow," he said, and a sob escaped his throat.

We all gasped in surprise. *Close the camp?*

"But we just got here!" Cranky Frankie called out. "Why are you closing the camp?"

Uncle Cousin cleared his throat again. "We are being shut down by the State Health Department," he replied.

"It seems that the beef stew Chef Indy served for dinner last night was actually sewage from the chemical-treatment plant down the street."

"GAAAACK!" Luke Puke jumped to his feet and ran for the bathroom.

"I scolded the chef for that," Cousin continued. "And he promised it probably wouldn't happen again." He sighed. "But the state is closing us down anyway.

"Does this mean we won't be able to go air horseback riding again?" Wacky Jackie asked.

"I'm afraid it does. We will just have time for our annual talent show," the camp headmaster replied.

"And, of course, we will name the Camp Champ Award winner after the show."

Patty Perfect jumped to her feet. "Peter and I want to thank you in advance for our award," she said. "We will be thrilled to be named Camp Champs tomorrow, in what will be our last and most glorious day here at Camp Lemme-Owttahere. Thank you all so *very* much!"

Peter Perfect stood up, and they both clapped for each other.

Adam Bomb leaned toward me and whispered, "We can still win the show tomorrow. *One* of us has to have talent—*right*?"

I shrugged. "Beats me."

THIRTY-SIX

Head Counselor Mama climbed onto the stage, tapping her cane in front of her. She had forgotten to brush her purple hair, and it stood out in all directions. It looked like her head was on fire.

Mama gazed down at us from the stage. "I know you cluck-clucks don't have any talent," she said. "But let's pretend."

She raised a notepad and a pen. "I'm sure you'll do your best tomorrow, which is pitiful and sad. But I say that out of love."

She reached out and smacked Pat Splat on the shoulder with her cane.

SMAAACK.

"Don't sit so close to the stage," she scolded.

Pat rubbed his shoulder. "**OWW.** Why did you do *that*?"

"Because I care," Mama said. "Now, listen up, you dit-dits."

"Booyah!" Uncle Cousin called from against the wall. "Plum pudding! Camp spirit, people! At least for one more day."

Mama raised her clipboard. "We need to plan the show. I'll go around the room. You tell me what your talent is."

Peter and Patty Perfect jumped to their feet again. "We have about a hundred talents," Patty said. "So we're going to perform them all."

"We're going to sing, dance, juggle, twirl batons, do a ventriloquist act, and perform magic tricks—*all at the same time*," Peter said.

They clapped for each other again.

"That sounds promising," Mama said.

Patty reached out her hands. "If you'd like to give us the Camp Champ trophy in advance, we'll be happy to accept it," she said.

"Let's wait," Mama said. "We'll give it to you tomorrow."

She then turned to the rest of us. "Any of you nut-whuts have a talent? Tell me what you can do so I can put it in the program."

Wacky Jackie raised her hand. "I can play the xylophone with my head," she said.

"Sorry," Mama said. "The camp doesn't have a xylophone." She squinted at Wacky Jackie. "Is there any other instrument you can play with your head?"

Jackie lowered her eyes to the floor. "No. Only the xylophone."

"Anyone else?" Mama asked, holding her pen over the notepad.

Rob Slob raised his hand. "I can burp a song I heard on WhoTube," he said.

Mama scribbled on her pad. "Excellent. That sounds like good entertainment." She raised her eyes to Rob. "What key do you burp in?"

"The key of B," Rob answered. "B for **BURRRRRRRP**."

"Anyone else?" Mama asked.

I raised my hand. "Here's my talent," I said. "I'd like to give a lecture on the history of nature."

"I don't think so," Mama said. "Next?"

Junkfood John raised his hand. "I can perform hip-hop beats," he said, "by chewing tortilla chips in a very loud rhythm."

"I didn't know you were musical," Mama said. She wrote it down on her notepad.

"I come from a musical family," John said. "My father wore a piano around the house."

Mama squinted at him. "He *wore* a piano? Why did he wear a piano?"

"The accordion didn't fit," John replied.

Mama turned to Nasty Nancy. "How about *you*?"

"What about me?" Nancy snapped.

"What's *your* talent?"

"I can do a stand-up comedy routine," Nancy said. "Here. I'll give you a sample of my jokes . . ."

She stepped onto the stage. "Good evening, ladies and jerks," she started. "What's green and purple and makes a frog look pretty? Your face! Hahaha. What's squishy like a rotten tomato and hard to look at? Your face! Ha ha. "What's yellow and wrinkled and shriveled up like a two-month-old lemon? Your face! Ha ha. What is—"

Mama raised her hand. "Hold it, hold it," she said. "Do all of your jokes end with *your face*?"

Nasty Nancy nodded. "You bet. I've got a *million* of them! What's red and sore and . . ."

"Not funny!" Mama exclaimed. "Your jokes aren't funny."

"Not as funny as *your face*!" Nancy exclaimed. "Hahaha."

"Where did you get those jokes?" Mama asked.

"From your face," Nancy replied.

Mama frowned at her. "What makes you think your jokes are funny?"

"Funny as your face?"

"I think you'd better rethink your jokes," Mama told her.

"You mean . . . rethink your face? Hahaha."

Mama let out a frustrated groan, smashed her cane over her knee, and broke it in half.

"Does that mean I'm not in the talent show?" Nasty Nancy asked.

Mama turned back to the rest of us. "Do any of you other nuk-nuks want to be in the show?"

Babbling Brooke raised her hand. "I'd like to perform a special camp cheer." She then jumped in the air, clapped her hands over her head, and began to cheer:

"GIVE ME AN L!

"GIVE ME AN E!

"GIVE ME AN M!

"GIVE ME ANOTHER M!

"GIVE ME AN E!

"GIVE ME AN O!

"GIVE ME A W!

"GIVE ME A T!

"GIVE ME ANOTHER T!

"GIVE ME . . . SOMETHING ELSE.

"GIVE ME ANOTHER LETTER.

"I LOST MY PLACE.

"I DON'T KNOW HOW TO SPELL THE NAME OF THIS CAMP.

"YAAAAY!"

Brooke clapped again. Then she did a high somersault in the air—

SPLAAAAAT.

—and landed on her head and didn't move.

"Someone carry this cheerleader to the nurse's cabin," Mama said. "I think we've had enough talent for one night. We'll figure out the show tomorrow."

Adam Bomb and Cranky Frankie carried Brooke away as Handy Sandy walked over to me. "Shhh, listen," she whispered. "I have a plan. I think one of us is going to win the talent show."

THIRTY-SEVEN

Handy Sandy led us to the side of the girls' cabin. She brought out a cardboard box, carrying it in front of her with both hands.

"EWWWW." Luke Puke pinched two fingers over his nose. "What smells so bad?"

"Your face?" Nasty Nancy said.

"Whoa. Smells like there was a skunk around here," I said.

"You're right," Handy Sandy said. She raised the box in front of her.

I pointed. "You have a skunk in that box?"

Sandy nodded.

"Why?" I demanded.

"It wouldn't fit in a bag," she said.

Leaky Lindsay sneezed.

"Are you allergic to skunks?" I asked.

"No," she said. "But I think I might be allergic to boxes. **AAAHCHOO!**"

Another strong gust of skunk smell floated over us. We all groaned and covered our noses.

"Where did you get the skunk?" Wacky Jackie asked.

"At the skunk store," Sandy replied, then laughed. "No, just joking. I found it in the woods."

"Most people think the skunk is a mammal," I said. "But it isn't. It's actually a legume."

"You're so smart, Janey," Sandy said. "But I'm the one with the awesome plan to keep the Perfect twins from winning the talent show."

"Let's hear it," I said.

"It's really quite simple," she said. "When Peter and Patty are onstage, showing off all their brilliant talents, I release the skunk."

"That's your plan?" Nasty Nancy asked. "Your *whole plan*?"

Handy Sandy nodded. "That's the whole plan. Peter and Patty will totally freak out. And the audience will go berserk." Sandy chuckled. "Everyone will panic and go nuts. The Perfects won't be able to finish their act. And one of us will have to be the winner."

"Brilliant!" Wacky Jackie gushed. "Brilliant!"

"Handy Sandy should be Camp Champ just for thinking of that plan!" Junkfood John exclaimed.

"I . . . can't . . . stand . . . the . . . stink . . . anymore!" Luke Puke choked out. He then ran around to the back of the cabin to throw up.

EXERCISES FOR SUMMER CAMP FROM COACH SWETTYPANTS

Listen up, everyone.

I'm Coach Swettypants, from Smellville Middle School.

While you are away at summer camp, you will want to keep up a good exercise program to stay in shape for camp activities.

Here are ten simple exercises you can do each morning before breakfast.

1. I call this one the One-Legged Jump Around.

It's really quite simple. When you get out of your bunk, stand solidly on the cabin floor. Then raise one foot in the air and begin to hop on the other foot. Ten hops in one direction, then ten hops back.

Let me demonstrate.

Two feet on the floor. Now, I raise my right leg and hold my knee up with both hands. And I begin to hop on my left foot.

One hop.

Two hops.

Ooooops.

Owwwwww.

Yikes!

I came down badly on that hop. Oh, wow. My ankle. I twisted it. It's *killing* me. I think I sprained it.

Whoa. Maybe it's broken. I can't stand on the foot. Can't put any weight on it.

I'm all alone in the gym here. Can you send someone to help me?

My ankle is starting to swell up like a balloon. Owwwwww.

I'm not good with pain. I admit it.

I'm trying not to cry.

Please, people—can anyone out there help me?

Forget the other nine exercises. I really need help.

Anyone? Is anyone out there?

THIRTY-EIGHT

Junkfood John here to report on the talent show.
We all jammed around the stage in the mess hall
to watch. I brought a lot of snacks with me because I
only had six cheeseburgers and a pizza for lunch, and
my stomach was still growling.

Unfortunately, I chew very loudly, so I couldn't

hear some of the music acts. I think Wacky Jackie did a wonderful harmonica number. Halfway through it, she swallowed the harmonica, though—so her number was pretty short. It's a good thing they didn't have an xylophone after all.

I'm sure she'll be okay after she gets her stomach pumped.

Rob Slob did an awesome act. He made balloon animals with only one balloon. They all ended up looking like worms, but they were terrific. We all wondered how he did it.

I went back to the cabin to get more snacks, so I missed Babbling Brooke's camp cheer and Nasty Nancy's comedy routine.

When I came back, Pat Splat was juggling these seriously heavy wooden duckpins. He tossed them in the air, and two of them landed on his head.

We had to take an intermission to carry him to the nurse.

I went back to the cabin because my snacks were running low. So I missed Adam Bomb's card tricks and Brainy Janey's lecture on the history of talent.

I asked Cranky Frankie if Janey's lecture was any good. But he said he forgot to listen.

Leaky Lindsay sang a medley of songs. I think the band was called Sneezer.

Luke Puke did a tap-dance to "America the Beautiful." But he was barefoot, so no one could hear his tapping.

The talent acts were all awesome. And I would have cheered for all of them if I didn't have my hands—and mouth—full of snacks.

Patty and Peter Perfect performed last. And of course we were all waiting for them to go onstage. Handy Sandy had the box with her smelly surprise hidden outside the mess hall. And we couldn't wait for her to bring it in and destroy the Perfects' act—and their chances of being Camp Champs.

Any second now, we were about to have a great victory. A moment we would never forget. It was the last day of camp, and we were about to have a memory that would last forever.

"Now it's time to bring out the winning act!" Head Counselor Mama announced from the stage. "Put your hands together for our winners—Peter and Patty Perfect!"

I didn't think that was fair. But there was no time to complain about it. Besides, we all knew that the Perfects' act would totally stink. Ha ha!

The room grew silent as Peter and Patty leaped onto the stage.

They were rollerblading on one leg and juggling batons high in the air.

Out of the corner of my eye, I saw Handy Sandy

leave the audience and sneak off to get the skunk box. I nearly choked on my Caramel Buffalo Pretzel Rods just thinking about what was about to happen.

Next, the Perfects did one hundred backflips and one hundred cartwheels in perfect unison. Then they began to tango to a flamenco song as they strummed on guitars.

The Perfects were still dancing and strumming as I saw Handy Sandy creep up to the side of the stage. She had the box between her hands, and I could tell she was trying hard not to laugh.

When Patty and Peter ended their dance and began to do another hundred cartwheels, Sandy lowered the box to the edge of the stage.

And lifted the lid.

Here we go! I said to myself.

THIRTY-NINE

No one made a sound. We all watched in silence, holding our breath, as the skunk slid out of the box and took a few steps across the stage. I even stopped chewing.

Peter and Patty put on top hats and began doing magic tricks. Neither of them saw the skunk as it crossed in front of them.

We weren't watching their magic tricks—all eyes were on the skunk.

Suddenly it made a sharp turn. And moved right toward the Perfects.

Peter Perfect pulled a stuffed rabbit from his top hat. He was expecting us all to applaud, but no one cared about his trick. We only cared about the skunk, which was scampering now, moving closer and closer.

And then it turned again.

Now the skunk was hurrying to the front of the stage—scurrying quickly toward us on the floor. No one moved. We had no idea what to expect next.

The next thing we knew, the animal *leaped* into the audience. And landed on Pat Splat, who had just returned from the nurse.

The skunk bounced off Pat's head and onto to the floor.

As we watched in shock, it lifted its tail and began to spray.

"EEWWWWWWW."

Horrified moans rang off the walls as the putrid odor floated over all of us. The smell burned my eyes, and I started to choke.

Spray after spray.

Everyone jumped to their feet, screaming and crying and groaning. You can guess what Luke Puke was doing.

I jumped up, too. And the odor jumped up with me. My clothes were soaked with skunk juice. I'll probably stink for the rest of my life.

I followed the others to the mess hall door. As I glanced back, I saw the skunk chasing after us!

Another spray. The stench was so heavy, I could feel it on my shoulders. Was that sweat pouring down my face, or was it skunk juice?

Choking and gagging, I raised my burning eyes to the stage. And gasped in shock.

FORTY

Patty and Peter Perfect were break dancing. They were rapping a fast beat and dancing to it on the stage.

They hadn't stopped their act! They were still *going!*

We all turned at the door and watched. I couldn't believe my eyes. Even a deadly stink attack by a crazed skunk couldn't stop the two of them!

Peter did a handstand. And Patty climbed up and balanced on the soles of his feet. "Ta-daa!" she cried.

"I . . . CAN'T . . . TAKE . . . IT . . . ANYMORE!" Adam Bomb screamed at the top of his voice. "WE NEVER GET A BREAK. WE NEVER WIN. THE PERFECTS ALWAYS WIN NO MATTER WHAT WE DO. I . . . CAN'T . . . STAND . . . IT!"

And once again, Adam Bomb exploded.

Pieces of our friend flew across the mess hall in all directions.

The explosion rocked the entire building. Everything shook—as if we were having a powerful earthquake.

The Perfect twins toppled off the stage. Then the stage collapsed, and they disappeared behind it.

The walls trembled, the floor pulsed and vibrated, and we were all thrown to the ground.

When things stopped, a hush fell over the mess hall. I climbed shakily to my feet and helped some of the other kids up.

The skunk gave us one more juicy spray, then disappeared out the open mess hall door.

"That plan didn't work too well," Handy Sandy said. "My bad."

"That plan didn't work too well," Handy Sandy said. "My bad."

We all struggled to catch our breath.

Uncle Cousin strode to the center of the room, shaking his head. He held a silver trophy in his hands. "I guess I have no choice," he said, and let out a long sigh.

"Booyah, everyone. Ricky ticky and booyah. This year's Camp Champ award goes to . . . *Nervous Rex*! He was the only one of you smart enough *not* to participate! Now can someone go to his cabin and take this trophy to him?"

R.L. STINE has more than 400 million English-language books in print, plus international editions in thirty-two languages, making him one of the most popular children's authors of all time. Besides Goosebumps, he has written series including Fear Street, Rotten School, Mostly Ghostly, the Nightmare Room, Dangerous Girls, and Just Beyond. Stine lives in New York City with his wife, Jane, an editor and publisher.

JEFF ZAPATA has worked on comic books and trading cards for more than twenty-five years, including thirteen gross, memorable ones as an editor, art director, and artist on Garbage Pail Kids and other brands at the Topps Company.

FRED WHEATON has been wallowing in the Garbage Pail at Topps since 2006, contributing disgusting concepts, final art, comics, and sketch cards. He lives in Washington, DC, with his wife and their three kids.

JOE SIMKO is an artist known for his happy-horror style. He is one of the premiere Garbage Pail Kids illustrators for the Topps Company and lives in New York City with his wife, son, dog, and many, many boxes of cereal.

THE TOPPS COMPANY, INC., originator of Garbage Pail Kids, Mars Attacks, and Bazooka Joe brands, was founded in 1938 and is the preeminent creator and marketer of physical and digital trading cards, entertainment products, and distinctive confectionery.

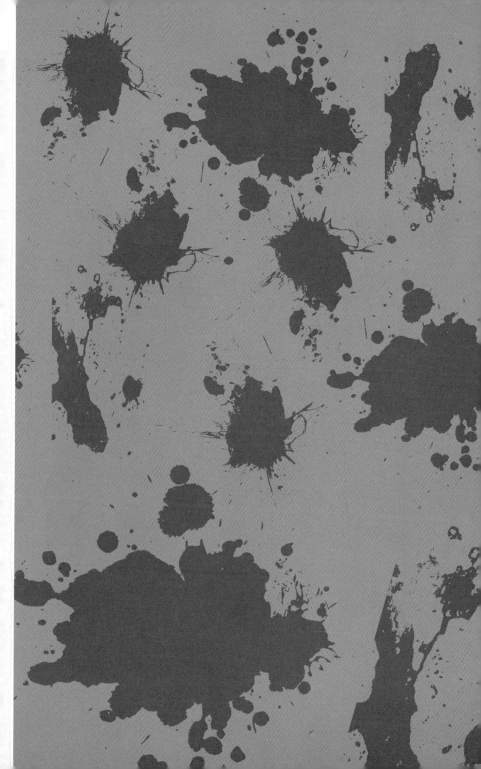